SPECIAL NEW AUTHORS' INTRODUCTION

Behind the New Direction

This book was written when three positions were generally considered acceptable in New York City: Left, lefter, and leftist. One of the authors went out with a young woman whose chilling left vision of the world seemed very much like Nazi Germany. The only difference was who would be going into the ovens. Most of the writers at the time considered left the direction of virtue, and were surprised how each country that was liberated, became a hell hole. You could tell the countries already "liberated." People would be shot for trying to leave, and the UN, and most of the press, would stop criticizing them.

In any case, this young woman with a dynamite body had a vision of an especially native socialism for America, a "Yankee Doodle Socialism," as she called it. The author asked her if she ever heard of "National Socialism." She hadn't.

"They were the Nazis," she was told.

"We'll be different."

"No you're not," the author told her.

"Then put on your pants and get out of here," she said.

"I was only joking," the author said. Then he began *Terror Squad*, which deals with revolutionary

groups. There was a special righteous irony in his writing. She didn't believe he was joking, and he did have to put on his pants. In that cold night, the true dangers of the international left were perceived, as the author bought a *Playboy* magazine and went home alone.

Message from Chiun

Here we have the second book dealing with Sinanju,* who I will not mention, although the authors' feel free to bandy about his name. And as an introduction, the author writes about his own pants.

Now these two, the authors, should disapprove once and for all the Darwinian theory of survival of the fittest. Could Sapir and Murphy be the fittest of anything? Even the fittest of whites?

What happened in this book is that Sinanju seduced unwitting people to his own ends. That is what happened in this book. What is left out of this book is the difficulty I had at that time, reasoning with Remo, whom many of you have been led to believe is white.

On this subject I will say only one thing. The authors are white. Does that lead you to believe there might be some hidden self interest here? The authors are the people who describe the characters in the book. You know what race they are by the way the authors describe them. This subject comes up again in later books. In those books, they imply

* The shame of Sinanju is Nuic. So evil was Nuic that Chiun reversed the sounds of his name so as to be the opposite of such infamy. Nuic was introduced in book seven.

that I, Chiun, Master of Sinanju, glory of the sun source of all the martial arts, would mislead you.

The real lies are these books. I am hard pressed to name one that fully and honestly portrays the glory of Sinanju. And since you seem like a nice person, let me confide in you, that you cannot get the glory of Sinanju in English. The language was meant for science, but not for the greater truths of how you breathe, move, and think.

English was never a language for breathing. Name one major work on how to breathe. Go into your library and find the breathing section. It is not there, not in an English library.

Therefore these books in English give you only a mild understanding of the true magnificence that is Sinanju. Sinanju, the glory of Sinanju, is the real reason these books sell, and can only be taught fully in pure Korean. I refer to the decent language before the modern corruptions from Pyong Yang or the evil Japanese influence, or the sloth of the Chinese tongue. I refer of course, to that awesome language of my ancestors.

You could have had it, by the way. I suggested giving the authors Sinanju in the only form it can be written, pure Korean using the Tang poem structure. It would have been a mere 12,000 pages, and by the end of it, you would have known the first simple elements of breathing, so you could stop doing it the way you and your ancestors have done it forever, any which way you happen to start the moment your backsides touched cold air.

No, they said. Twelve thousand pages was too long. Too long? Do you know how many pages these books add up to so far? Fifteen thousand at least. And much of it has to do with violence, and whites. Is that Sinanju? Is that what you have paid so much money for?

And now you are paying again. More. For what you could have gotten for less years ago. No wonder twenty-four million copies of these things have sold.

To this civilization, the authors imply, I, Chiun, would bother to lie. Shame on them. And you. If you believe it. Go read about people putting their pants back on.

MURPHY & SAPIR

AUTHORS' CHOICE

BEST OF

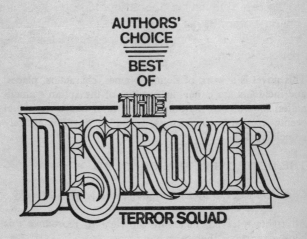

THE DESTROYER

TERROR SQUAD

PINNACLE BOOKS   **NEW YORK**

TO:
Graces

THE DESTROYER: TERROR SQUAD

Copyright © 1973 by Richard Sapir and Warren Murphy

An original Pinnacle Books edition.

First printing/June 1973

ISBN: 0-523-42415-9
Can. ISBN: 0-523-43405-7

Printed in the United States of America

PINNACLE BOOKS, INC.
1430 Broadway
New York, New York 10018

18 17 16 15 14 13 12 11 10 9

CHAPTER ONE

An airplane is an unsupportable outpost. You cannot reinforce it. You cannot resupply it.

Mrs. Kathy Miller listened to this description on a flight from New York City to Athens, Greece. The man beside her was fascinating, a gentle person in his late thirties with soft brown eyes and a craggy face honed by wind and sun. He spoke with a slightly guttural accent she could not place, and he was attempting, unsuccessfully, to calm her fears about skyjacking.

"Airplane travel today is far safer than going from one small village to another during the Middle Ages." he said. "And for the hijacker, it is becoming almost impossible today to successfully achieve the capture of a plane. It is a vulnerable, unreinforceable outpost in the air. It has to land."

He smiled. Mrs. Miller hugged her infant son Kevin closer to her breast. She was not reassured.

"If worse comes to worst, we will all fly around and land in perhaps Libya or Cairo and then be returned. Even the most militant governments today are tired of hijackers. So, I do not know how horrible a delay would be for you, but for me it would be delightful. I have you and your adorable child for company. Americans are such good people, really."

"I hate the idea of hijacking. Even the thought of it makes me . . . well, mad and frightened."

"Ah, so we have it, Mrs. Miller. You are not afraid

7

of the hijacking, but the idea of it. Being defenseless."

"Yes. I guess so. I mean, what right do those people have to endanger my life? I never did anything to anyone."

"A mad dog, Mrs. Miller, does not dispense justice. Let us be grateful that their fangs are weak."

"How can you say they're weak?"

"How can you say they're strong?"

"Very simply. They kill people. They murdered those athletes in Munich, those diplomats in wherever-it-was. They shoot people from rooftops. They bomb stores. They snipe at innocent people from hotel rooms. I mean, that isn't weak."

The passenger in the next seat chuckled.

"That is the sign of weakness. Strength is irrigating a field. Strength is constructing a building. Strength is discovering a cure for a disease. The random lunatic killing of a few people here and there is not strength. The odds against getting hurt by those madmen are astronomical."

"But it can happen," said Kathy Miller. She felt strangely annoyed by the man's argument. Why did he take terrorism so lightly? Her fear was gone now. It had been replaced by annoyance.

"Many things can happen," he said. "But that's life. Landslides when you ski. Sharks when you swim. Accidents when you drive. But to live life, you must accept accidents as such, as inherent parts of living. You see, what bothers you is the fact that you are vulnerable to accidents, not that accidents exist. What bothers you is that these terrorists remind you of something you would like to keep hidden in some dark closet. Your mortality.

"The answer to these mad animals is to live. To love. Look, you have a beautiful baby. You are going to meet your husband in Athens. Your very life and loving is a refutation, and a strong refutation, of every terrorist act ever committed. You are taking an airplane today. That shows the terrorists are weak. They could not stop you."

"There's something wrong with that argument," said Kathy Miller. "I don't know how or why, but there's something wrong."

A stewardess leaned over the three-seat section and, with a plastic smile, asked if anyone wanted a beverage.

Mrs. Miller wanted a cola.

Her neighboring passenger shook his head.

"Pure sugar and caffeine," he said. "No good for you or for your baby whom you breastfeed."

"How do you know he's not on a bottle?"

"Just the way you hold him, Mrs. Miller. My wife also. I know. That's all."

"I love cola," she said.

Three men in business suits brushed quickly behind the stewardess, heading toward the front of the plane. The passenger, whose movements had been so slow and relaxed, looked up suddenly at the three men, watching them like a gazelle alert for a tiger.

"Do you have the cola now?" he asked the stewardess.

Kathy Miller blinked in puzzlement. What was going on?

"Yes. I have it right on this cart," said the stew.

"Now, please," said the passenger.

"Two colas then," said the stewardess.

The passenger, who had been so gentle and consider-

9

ate since the plane left New York City, rudely snatched a drink before the stewardess could serve Kathy.

He held it to his lips, watching the front of the plane in wide-eyed fear. Kathy could see he held a white oblong pill near the lip of the glass.

Without taking his eyes off the front of the plane, he said: "I want you to remember one thing, Mrs. Miller. Love is always stronger. Love is strength. Hate is weakness."

Kathy Miller did not have time for philosophy. Over the plane's loudspeaker came words that curdled her intestines.

"This is the Revolutionary Liberation Front of Free Palestine. Through our courageous endeavors, we have gloriously captured this vehicle of capitalistic-zionistic oppression. We have liberated this airplane. It is now in our hands. Make no sudden moves and you will not be hurt. Any sudden moves and you will be shot. Everyone put his hands on his head. No sudden moves. Anyone who fails to put his hands on his head will be shot."

To put her hands on her head would mean dropping the baby. Kathy Miller put her left hand on her head and held the baby with her right. Maybe one hand would be good enough. She shut her eyes and prayed, prayed as she had been taught to pray in Sunday School in Eureka, Kansas. She talked to God, explaining that she had nothing to do with this and that they shouldn't hurt her or the baby. She begged God to let her and her baby live.

"Dr. Geleth. Dr. Isadore Geleth. In which seat are you?" came the voice over the loudspeaker.

Kathy could hear people move down the aisle. She

felt a wetness at her feet. It must be her cola, that she had dropped. She did not want to open her eyes to see it, though. She would keep her eyes shut and hold Kevin to her chest and it would all pass. She had nothing to do with this whole thing. She was just a passenger. At worst, the plane would fly around a few hours longer and then she would open her eyes and find that they had finally landed at Athens Airport. That's what would happen if she kept her eyes shut. The people who were hijacking the plane would have to land somewhere. They would get off and she and Kevin would fly with everyone else to Athens.

"Dr. Geleth. We know you are aboard. We will find you, Dr. Geleth. Do not endanger other passengers," said the voice from the loudspeaker.

Kathy heard the passengers murmur. One woman shouted that she was having a heart attack. A young child cried. A stewardess kept repeating that everyone should be calm. Kathy felt the plane descend. She remembered she had read somewhere that a bullet through the skin of a plane at high altitude could cause an explosion. Or was it an implosion? No, an explosion. Everything would rush out. Air pressure at high altitudes made a gun battle tantamount to turning the aircraft into a bomb.

"Dr. Geleth. We will get you. We call upon the passengers to signal if they are sitting next to Dr. Geleth or know where he is. We do not wish to harm you. We are peaceful. We do not wish to harm anyone."

Kathy felt something hard and metallic next to her head.

"I can't put my other hand up. I'll drop my baby," she said.

"Open your eyes." The voice was soft and menacing, the silky smoothness of a snake.

Kathy did what she had not wished to do until it was all over. She opened her eyes. A pistol was pointed at her forehead, and a nervous, gaunt-faced young man in a business suit leaned over from the aisle holding it.

The passenger who had assured her that hijacking was so improbable was sleeping through this. His eyes were closed, his hands relaxed on his lap. The tip of his tongue stuck out of his lips like a sliver of bubble gum. It was then that Kathy realized that she was still holding her drink, in the hand above her head. The passenger had dropped his and that was probably the wetness she had felt. But she did not dare look down.

"You know him?" said the gunman, nodding toward the passenger.

"No. No. We just talked," said Kathy.

"We know him," said the gunman, and let out a stream of foreign words that sounded as if he were preparing to spit.

Quickly another gunman came up behind him in support.

"May I put down my drink?" asked Kathy. The other gunman, a swarthy youth with the inner stillness of a cave, nodded that she might do so.

Kathy dropped the drink to the carpeted floor of the plane and clutched Kevin with both hands.

"What is your name, if you please?" asked the swarthy gunman.

"Miller. Mrs. Katherine Miller. My husband is an

12

engineer for a construction firm. He's on a job in Athens. I'm flying there to meet him."

"Very good. And what did Dr. Geleth say to you while you flew next to each other?"

"Oh, just conversation. I don't know him. I mean, we just talked." She kept waiting for the passenger to wake up, to say something, to draw their attention from her onto himself.

"I see," the gunman said. "And he gave you something?"

"No, no," said Kathy, shaking her head. "He didn't give me anything."

The swarthy gunman gave a sharp command in that guttural language. The gun next to Kathy's head disappeared inside a belt. His hands free, the lighter-skinned gunman removed the jacket from Dr. Geleth and in the leaden way the body responded, Kathy knew the gentle passenger next to her was dead. The pill he had held near his glass when the three men in business suits went forward, had obviously been poison.

With swift expert hands, the lighter gunman stripped and searched Dr. Geleth.

"Nothing," he said finally.

"No matter. It was his mind that we wanted. Mrs. Miller, are you sure Dr. Geleth said nothing of importance to you?"

Kathy shook her head.

"Let us try. What were the last words he said to you?"

"He said love was stronger than hate."

"That is a lie. He told you something," said the swarthy gunman, his lips quivering.

13

"We have failed," said the lighter-skinned man. "What could he tell her in a minute? Besides, even if he had given her his life's work, what was important was him. His body for ransom. He knew that dead, he was worth nothing to us in an exchange. We are defeated. We failed."

Froth formed at the corner of the swarthy man's mouth.

"We have not failed. This American helped the Jew. If the Americans didn't help, we would have succeeded. She is responsible."

"Brother, leader. She is just a housewife."

"She knows something. She is part of the capitalistic-zionistic plot that cheated us of victory."

"Dr. Geleth cheated us, not her."

The swarthy face reddened and the dark eyes heated with anger.

"You sound like an Israeli agent. One more defeatist word and I will shoot you. Take her and the child to the rear. I will question them."

"Yes, brother leader."

Kathy tried to get up but something held her down. The lighter-skinned gunman reached over and she thought he was going to touch her private parts, but he merely unbuckled the seat belt.

He helped Kathy to her feet and she stumbled into the aisle over the legs of Dr. Geleth.

"I really didn't know him," she sobbed.

"It wouldn't have made any difference if you did," said the light gunman. "He was not military. He was just valuable for what he was."

"What was he?" asked Kathy.

"Cancer research. We do not want the Israelis to be

14

the first to discover a cure. It would be too good for their propaganda. But we would have been willing to trade back Geleth for some of our members in Israeli jails."

"Quiet!" came the command from the leader.

In the rear lounge, the leader took Kevin from Kathy.

"Search her," he said to his accomplice. There was a stream of the spitting language which Kathy now judged to be Arabic. It came from the lighter gunman. He said it with palm open, as if disputing the sanity of the order. A quick violent sentence from the leader and the other gunman bowed his head.

"Strip," he said, "I'm going to search you."

Sobbing, Kathy took off her plaid jacket and white blouse and unzippered her skirt. She let it fall to her ankles. She averted her eyes from theirs.

"Strip, he said," barked the leader. "He did not mean leave clothing. Strip is strip."

Head bowed, Kathy reached behind her back and unhitched her bra. She was too terrified now for shame. She jimmied the panties down from her hips and let them fall along her legs over the skirt at her feet.

"Search her whole body," said the leader. "With your hands."

"Yes, Mahmoud," said the lighter gunman.

"Do not use names," said the leader, Mahmoud.

Her eyes shut, Kathy felt the hands brush her shoulder and armpits and backside. The hands were brisk.

"All the parts," said Mahmoud.

Kathy felt the hands linger over her breasts, and although she did not want it to happen, her breasts responded. The hands moved away down her sides, and then at first harshly, then softly, then not harshly

15

enough, a hand invaded her body. And her body betrayed her. While her mind said "no," her body said "yes."

She kept her eyes closed when she was taken and in her mind told her husband that she was sorry. She felt triumphant that she was not able to move with her ravisher. She remained stiff on the lounge sofa and then the intrusion was gone, followed almost immediately by another intrusion. Another hijacker was taking her. This time it hurt. And by the third, she was in great pain.

When they were through with her, they dumped her into the bathroom and locked it. She could feel the plane hit turbulence and kept telling herself that the unsupportable outpost would have to land somewhere. It was cold in the plane's bathroom and she tried to cover herself with hand towels. She felt broken and worthless and used, yet she knew she had done nothing wrong. She couldn't help herself.

She knocked on the door. Nothing. She knocked again. Nothing.

"Please, my baby. My baby. At least give me back my baby."

Nothing. So she banged harder and then banged continuously.

"Quiet," came the harsh command.

"My baby. My baby," she whimpered.

"Quiet."

She could hear crying outside, a baby's crying. It was Kevin.

"My baby," she yelled. "Damn you bastards. Give me back my baby, you damned bastards. Animal bastards. Give me back my baby."

Suddenly the crying ceased. The door unlocked and a white object came hurtling at her head. Instinctively, she ducked it and then was immediately sorry. It hit the lavatory wall and rebounded down toward the toilet. Kathy desperately grabbed Kevin's chest and plucked him from the water. As soon as she saw his head wobble to the side, she knew she was too late. She had been too late when the door had opened. A large reddish welt rose from the neck and Kevin's pink head dangled crazily over his chest. They had broken his neck before they threw him in.

When the unsupportable outpost finally did land, Mrs. Kathy Miller was still hugging the body of her baby. But now Kevin was cold and her breasts were hurting, with the force of the now-unneeded milk.

The hijackers were greeted by an Arab honor guard and praised for their heroism, and their role in writing "another glorious chapter in Arab courage, honor and daring, part of a thousand years of similar achievement by the courageous Arab peoples. This wondrous act, oh heroes of the Arab liberation struggle, typifies the very spirit of the Arab peoples in their unquenchable yearning for glory and honor and justice."

When all the passengers finally reached Athens, Arab spokesmen and their supporters were already giving out stories about the death of the Miller baby. Some said the mother, in a fit of hysteria caused by the pilot, killed her own child. Others said while they would not say whether or not they approved the killing of the baby, they understood the reasons "why men were driven to do things like this." They spoke softly to the newsmen in the same spitting accents of the hijackers.

Many living rooms around the world watched the

explanations, and watched the haggard, drawn faces of the passengers finally departing from the plane in Athens.

In one room, the lapping of waves outside could be heard. There was no shock on the faces of the three men watching the television set. All were in their late forties and wore suits and ties. All three held the rank of colonel, but in three different services—American, Russian and Chinese.

They watched the Miller woman, her emotions smothered by shock's blanket, softly describe the rape, then the death of her baby.

"Chickenshit," said the American. "Real chickenshit. Rape and baby killing."

"That's what worries me," said the Chinese colonel.

"The rape of a woman? And the death of a baby?" asked the Russian colonel. He was incredulous. He knew Colonel Huang had witnessed countless atrocities by the Japanese and by war lords; and while all three men found the killing of non-combatants distasteful, it was not a shocking tragedy to end the world. It wasn't even a military situation to be given any constructive thought. It was as if a dog had been run over on a highway. Too bad, but you didn't rearrange the highways of the world because of it.

"Yes, it worries me," said Colonel Huang. He turned off the television set and glanced out the porthole at the calm water extending out to the reddening horizon. There was nothing so secure as an American navy vessel on the high seas, to accomplish sensitive international arrangements without interruption.

"It worries me," continued Colonel Huang, sitting

18

down at the table with the other two colonels, "when undisciplined operatives can pull off a hijacking that efficiently."

"He's right," said Colonel Anderson. "We didn't have an easy problem to begin with, Petrovich. We just may be up against something that is going to be impossible."

"Worry, worry, worry. First of all, how do you know the operatives were undisciplined, as you say? When we entered Berlin, we had those problems too."

"Not from your top troops. Your stragglers, Petrovich. Elite units don't rape or kill babies. Come on."

"So. One isolated incident," said Colonel Petrovich testily. He threw up his hands as if it were nothing.

"No, it's not," said Colonel Anderson. "It's a pattern. A splinter group of the IRA takes out an entire wing of British Army headquarters and stops to hold up a department store. A unit of the South American Tupemaros goes crazy in a girl's school, yet still manages to cut its way through a full, well-armored division of the Venezuelan Army."

"You know it was full armored?" asked Colonel Huang.

"Yes," Anderson said quickly, "I know. For a fact. Now the important thing is that the United Nations conference on terrorism is going to start next week. And we have to have our international agreements worked out by that time. Let's face it. We wouldn't be here at all, if our governments didn't feel it was in their own best interests to stop terrorism once and for all."

The other two colonels nodded solemnly, then Petrovich said, "And we have done very well. We have worked out all kinds of technical problems in these last few weeks. Next week, our governments will jointly present our plan to eliminate terrorism, and all the other nations will go along because they will think they participated in the debate. So why do we worry now?"

"Colonel," Anderson said stiffly, "we have worked out pretty-solid agreements here on arms, skyjacking, random violence, and political kidnaping. But this new wave of terrorism may contain a new ingredient that makes our work a waste of time."

Colonel Huang nodded. Petrovich shrugged. Were they both going mad?

"All our work has been built on the need to cut off terrorist groups from a base. We've presumed that they need training; they need financing; they need a country to work from. But what if they don't?"

"Impossible," Petrovich said.

"No, it's not," Anderson said.

"He's right," said Huang. "That hijacking was pulled off slickly by people who obviously had no training or discipline. The British outpost was levelled by little more than street hoodlums. The guerillas in Venezuela were common field hands out on a lark. Somehow, somewhere, in the last two weeks, the whole nature of terrorism has changed. Don't you see, Petrovich, it is no longer tied to a country? And if that is so, the agreements we work out here for the world are worthless." Huang sat back in his chair.

Anderson nodded, then added: "Do you realize those skyjackers got their weapons past the very latest metal detection devices? And they took over the plane in thirty-seven seconds?"

"Competence," said Colonel Petrovich. "Just competence."

"Instant military competence for anyone," Huang corrected. "And that is what is so frightening."

"And against *that* kind of competence," Anderson said, "sanctions are useless, because this new wave of terrorism does not need a host country to train in."

"We can't be sure of that," Petrovich said. "All terrorists are cow dung at heart. I can't be sure that these incidents prove they have access to instant training."

"Well, that is what I plan to report to my government," Anderson said. "And I would suggest that both of you report the same thing to your superiors: that we believe there is a new movement underway in terrorism and that the conference will be useless unless we can figure out what this new force is and how to handle it."

Colonel Anderson felt sure that the American government would appreciate the soundness of his thinking. He had good lines right up to the top. It was a shock, therefore, when he heard the reaction to his report two days later in the Pentagon.

"It is the policy of our government to proceed as if no new terrorist force exists," said the President's personal military advisor, Lt. Gen. Charles Whitmore.

"C'mon, Chuck—are you out of your head?" asked Anderson.

"The United States government, Colonel, will submit, in conjunction with China and the Soviet Union, a plan to control terrorism. This plan will be advanced next week. You and your two associates will continue working out the final details."

Anderson rose from his seat. "Are you people crazy, Chuck?" He slammed his fist down on the broad, highly polished desk that was bare, but for a flag with three stars. "That conference won't mean a spit in a windstorm unless we have some kind of good handle on this new force. All the talk you want, all the sanctions you want, they won't mean a goddam thing and we'll be right back where we started from. Even worse, 'cause the sanctions won't work, and we'll have a harder time getting them next time around."

"Colonel, I don't know how much of your military etiquette you remember from the Point, but desk banging by a colonel on a lieutenant general's desk is not proper military protocol."

"Protocol, my ass, Chuck. That's for the troops. We've got a problem and you're sticking your head in the sand."

"Colonel, it may interest you to know that I relayed your message verbatim. It may possibly interest you to know that I yelled also. I may have yelled myself out of my career, but, Colonel, yell I did. And I was told, Colonel, by my superior that I should relay to you that we will proceed with the conference as if this new terrorist force does not exist. It was an order from my Commander in Chief. It was a direct order. To be followed, Colonel."

Colonel Anderson sat back in his chair. He was quiet for a few long seconds, and then he grinned.

"Okay, Chuck, what is it? The CIA?"

"I don't know what you mean, Colonel."

"Dammit, Chuck, don't be cute with me. I have to deal with Petrovich and Huang and I need answers. Look, the President's no fool. You've explained the whole thing to him. He says, business as usual. To me, that can mean only one thing. He thinks he's going to

22

have this new terrorist force pinned down by next week. So, now I ask, is the CIA going to do it?"

"Colonel, I assure you, I have no idea."

"Have if your own way, Chuck," said Anderson, getting to his feet. "But I wish you'd pass along one message if you could. This new terrorist force is something special. I don't think the CIA's good enough to handle it. But that's the President's problem, not mine. Just, when you get involved in it, you tell whoever's in charge that they better work hard and make no mistakes. These people are good."

"Thank you, Colonel," said General Whitmore, indicating the meeting was over. He stayed at his desk, staring at the door which closed behind Anderson. The President just had not seemed concerned about the new terrorist force, and when Whitmore had suggested the CIA, the President had jumped down his throat. "No CIA," he had said. "I'll handle this."

The President had seemed almost cocky about it, almost as if he had some kind of special force that Whitmore knew nothing about. The general bent over his desk and doodled on the blotter. He agreed with Anderson. These new terrorists were serious. The President's special force had better be something really special.

CHAPTER TWO

His name was Remo, and he did not feel very special.

He felt incredibly ordinary that bright California morning, standing beside his sky-blue pool, just like any other pool, near any other luxury villa in this luxury community in a luxury county where everyone talked about his stock investments, or the movie he was making, or the bitch of an income tax.

Did Remo find the new tax bill threatening? He was asked this often at the ordinary cocktail parties made ordinary by their repetition and the dull ordinariness of the people attending them who invariably felt, for some strange reason, that they were extraordinary.

No, Remo did not find the new tax bill threatening.

Would Remo care for a cocktail? A joint? A pill?

No, Remo did not indulge.

An hors d'oeuvre?

No, it might have monosodium glutamate and Remo ate only once a day anyhow.

Was Remo a health food addict?

No, his body was.

The face was familiar. Did Remo make a flick in Paris?

No. Perhaps they just used the same plastic surgeon.

Just what did Remo do for a living?

Suffered fools gladly.

Would Remo care to repeat that statement out on the terrace?

Not really.

Did Remo know he was speaking to the former amateur light heavyweight champion of California and a black belt holder, not to mention the heavy mob connections anyone owning a studio would have?

Remo did not realize all that.

Would Remo care to repeat that statement about fools?

The fool had done it for him.

How would Remo like an hors d'oeuvre in his face?

That would be quite impossible because the silver hors d'oeuvre tray was going to be wrapped around the fool's head.

Remo remembered that last cocktail party he had attended in Beverly Hills, how two servants had to hammer and chisel the tray from the movie mogul's head, how the movie mogul complained directly to Washington, even used his influence to get government agencies to check out Remo's background. They found nothing, of course. Not even a Social Security number. Which was natural. Dead men have neither Social Security numbers nor fingerprints on file.

Remo stuck a toe into the too-blue water. Lukewarm. He glanced back at the house where the wide glass patio doors were open. He heard the morning soap operas grinding into their teary beginnings. Suddenly a voice cut through the television organ music.

"Are you ready? I'll be listening," came a squeaky, Oriental voice from inside the house.

"Not ready yet, little father," said Remo.

"You should always be ready."

"Yeah. Well, I'm not," yelled Remo.

"A wonderful answer. A full explanation. A rational cause."

"Well, I'm just not ready yet. That's all."

". . . for a white man," came the squeaky Oriental voice.

"For a white man," hissed Remo testily under his breath.

He tried the water with the other foot. Still lukewarm. There had been flack from headquarters over the hors d'oeuvre tray incident.

Was Remo aware of the incredible jeopardy he had placed the agency in by attracting attention?

Remo was aware.

Did Remo know the effect on the nation if the existence of the agency should become known?

Remo knew.

Did Remo know the expense and risk the agency had gone to in establishing him as a man without living identity?

If Dr. Harold W. Smith, head of CURE, was referring to framing a policeman named Remo Williams for murder, getting the policeman sentenced to the electric chair so that when the switch was pulled and the body pronounced dead, the prints would be destroyed and the Social Security number removed, and the poor guy would no longer exist, if that's what Dr. Smith meant, yes, Remo remembered very well all the trouble CURE had gone to.

And all the trouble with the never-ending training that had turned him into something other than a normal human being, Remo remembered well.

He remembered a lot of things. Believing he was going to be executed and waking up in a hospital bed. Being told that the Constitution was in peril and a President had authorized an agency to have powers to fight crime beyond constitutional limits. A secret organization that would not exist. Only the President; Dr. Harold W. Smith, the head of the secret organization CURE; the recruiter; and Remo would ever know. And of course Remo was a dead man, having been executed the night before for murder.

Still, there had been a little problem when the recruiter got injured and lay drugged in a hospital bed, perhaps ready in his narcotic fog to talk about CURE. But that little matter was easily taken care of. Remo, the dead policeman, was ordered to kill him and then there were only three people who knew of CURE.

Why only one man for the enforcement arm of CURE? the ex-Remo Williams had asked.

Less chance of CURE becoming a threat to the government. Of course, the one man would get special training.

And he did—training from the Master of the House of Sinanju, training so extreme at times that even a real death seemed preferable.

Yes, Remo remembered all the trouble CURE had gone to for him, and if wrapping a tray around a fool's head endangered all that work, well, that was the business, sweetheart.

"Is that all you can say, Remo? That's the biz?" Dr. Smith had said in one of those rare face-to-face meetings.

"That's all I can say."

"Well, it's done," said the lemon-faced Dr. Smith. "Now to the business at hand. What do you know about terrorists?" Then followed an afternoon briefing on terrorists, a preamble to a mission.

Remo bent over and tinkled a hand in the pool like everyone else's pool in this luxury community.

"I do not hear a body move through the water," came the Oriental voice.

"I do not hear a body move through the water," Remo mimicked under his breath. He stood in boxer bathing trunks, an apparently normally built man in his early thirties with sharp features and deep dark eyes. Only his thick wrists would give any indication that this was more than an ordinary man, for the real deadliness was where it always is with man, in his mind.

"I do not hear a body move through the water," came the voice again.

Remo went into the pool. Not in a dive or a splashing jump, but instead, the way he had been taught, like the essence of gravity returning toward the center of the earth. Even a novice in the martial arts knew that collapsing was actually the fastest way of getting down. This was an extension of it. One moment, Remo was standing on the side of the pool, and the next, the luke-warm water surrounded him, above him, and around him, and his feet were on tile. To someone watching, it would appear as if the pool just sucked him in.

He waited, letting his eyes adjust to the stinging chlorinated water, letting his restricted use of oxygen adjust his body, letting the arms float while the mind concentrated the focus of the weight at his feet and legs to keep him steady underwater.

He was in a world of warm blue jade and he adjusted to become part of it, not fight it. When he had first learned moving through water, he had tried harder and harder, and succeeded less and less. The Master of Sinanju, Chiun, had said that when he stopped trying he would learn to move through water, and that it was Remo's arrogance that made him believe he could overpower it, instead of submitting to it.

"By submission, you conquer," Chiun had said, and then demonstrated.

The wisp of an aged Oriental had entered the water properly, leaving a trail of only three small bubbles following the descent of his body, as if a small rock had been placed gently, not dropped, into the water. Without seeming propulsion, the body suddenly was moving through the water much as Remo had seen a tiger shark do in a city aquarium back east. No flailing. No straining. Swish. Swish. Swish. And Chiun was at the other end of the pool and out of the water as though vacuumed out. It was the training of the House of Sinanju that made its masters appear not to push themselves but to be pulled.

Remo had tried. Failed. Tried again. Failed. Until one tired afternoon, following three failures in which he had moved no better than an ordinary swimmer, he felt the tuning of his body.

His body in conjunction with the water made the forward movement. It was too easy to believe. And then, trying it again, he found he could not do it again.

Chiun had leaned over the pool and taken Remo's hand. He pushed it against the water. Remo felt force. Then he pulled Remo's hand through the water. The hand moved swiftly, without effort. The water accepted the hand.

That was the key.

"Why didn't you show me this the first time?" Remo had asked.

"Because you did not know what you did not know. You had to begin at ignorance."

"Little father," Remo had said, "you're as clear as scripture."

"But your testaments are not clear at all," Chiun had said. "And I am very clear. Unfortunately, a light to a blind man is always inadequate. You now know how to move through water."

And Chiun was right. Remo never failed again. Now, as he unweighted his feet, he understood the water, its very nature, and he too moved, not cutting through but blending the weight thrusts of his body with the mass of the water to pull himself forward. Swish. Swish. Swish. Up and out of the pool, then stroll back, leaving wet footprints on the yellow outdoor rug. It was not exercise, because exercise meant straining the body. This was practice.

Once more, down into the pool and off—swish, swish, swish. Then up and out and pad back to the beginning. On the third time, Remo glanced quickly back to the house. Competence had already brought him to the point of boredom. To hell with it. He slapped the water once at one end, dashed to the other and slapped it again.

"Perfect," came the Oriental voice. "Perfect. The first time you have achieved perfection. For a white man, that is."

It was only that evening when Chiun's television shows were over, and Remo continued to maintain a happy little secret smile, that Chiun looked quizzically at his pupil and said:

"That third moving through the water was false."

"What, little father?"

"False. You cheated."

"Would I do that?" asked Remo indignantly.

"Would the spring rice swallow the dew of the Yacca bird?"

"Would it? I don't know," Remo said. "I never heard of a Yacca bird."

"You know. You cheated. You are too happy for having paid the proper effort in this morning's training. But I say to you, whoever robs from his own efforts robs himself. And in our craft, the robber's price can well be death."

The telephone rang, interrupting the aged Oriental. Chiun, casting a baleful eye upon the ringing instrument, became quiet, as if unwilling to compete with a machine so insolent it would dare interrupt him. Remo picked up the receiver.

"This is Western Union," came the voice. "Your Aunt Alice is coming to visit you and wants you to prepare the guest room."

"Right," Remo said. "But what color guest room?"

"Just the guest room."

"Are you sure?"

"That's what it says, sir," said the Western Union operator, with the smug arrogance of one observing another's discomfort.

"Just guest room. Not blue guest room or red guest room?"

"Correct, sir. I will read. . . ."

Remo hung up on the Western Union operator, waited the few moments necessary for a dial tone, then dialed again, an 800 area-code number that he was ordered to call because the telegram did not mention the guest room's color.

The phone barely rang once and was answered.

"Remo, we're in luck. We got them 2,000 feet over Utah. Remo, this is you, right?"

"Well, yes it is. It would help to have you verify before you start vomiting over an open line. What the hell is the matter with you, Smitty?" Remo was shocked. Smith's external composure was usually perfect, almost Korean.

"We got a whole crew of them over Utah. They want ransom money. Federal agencies are negotiating now. The money delivery will be at Los Angeles Airport. See an FBI field representative, Peterson. He's a black man. You will be the negotiator. Jump the line to the top. This is the first lead we've had. Repeat for verify."

"See Peterson at Los Angeles Airport. Board the plane and try to find out who the leaders are of this whole thing. I assume this is an airline hijacking," Remo said drily.

"Beautiful. Get going now. You may not have time to lose."

Remo hung up.

"What is the matter?" asked Chiun.

"Dr. Harold Smith, our employer, has taken a mental leap off a cliff. I don't know what's the matter," said Remo, his face twisted in concern.

"You'll be working tonight, then?" Chiun said.

"Ummmm," said Remo, signifying assent. "Gotta go now."

"Wait. I might go with you. It might be a nice evening."

"Barbra Streisand's on tonight, Chiun."

"This thing you do cannot be done tomorrow night?"

32

"No."

"Good luck. And remember when you are tempted to take risks, think of all the hours I have invested in you. Think of the nothing you were and the level to which I have raised you."

"I'm pretty good, huh, little father?" said Remo, regretting the comment as soon as he made it.

"For a white man," Chiun said happily.

"Your mother is a Wasoo," yelled Remo, dashing out the door. He was across the yard and into the garage before he realized the Master of Sinanju was not chasing him. He did not know what a Wasoo was, but Chiun had used the word once in a very rare moment of anger.

The Rolls Royce Silver Cloud was the car parked closest to the garage door. It didn't really matter which car Remo drove or even owned. He didn't own anything. He only used things. He didn't even own his face which, every so often, especially if anyone should accidentally get a photograph, was changed by plastic surgery. He owned nothing and had the use of practically anything he wanted. Like the Rolls Royce, he thought, backing up the Silver Cloud, its magnificently honed motor humming quietly, moving effortlessly, a paramount achievement in its field—like Remo, the Destroyer, a testimonial to manufacturing skills.

As usual, the airport traffic was insufferable, but that was America and there were some things even training couldn't overcome. Unless, of course, he wanted to run over car roofs to get to the airport. He watched the sun set bloody red through its filter of pollution and knew that somewhere above him an airplane was heading for Los Angeles Airport with terrified people on board, being held as hostages by the hijackers. To some people it was a moment of terror. To the professional, it was only a link in a chain, and Remo was a professional. His assignment was to jump the line to the top. That meant, move into the terrorists' system and kill his way to the top, destroying the system. And his way into the system might be circling the airport at this very moment.

Remo honked the horn of the Rolls, a clear, resonant sound that did absolutely nothing to the clog of cars except instigate more horn honking. America. Remo wasn't sure sometimes why Smith was so gung ho to save it. What was even more puzzling was Smith's current strange excitement about the terrorists, even to the point of babbling on an open line. If they were as much a danger as Smith obviously thought, then it was even more important that CURE be careful. More reason to be calm. But then, something had felt wrong with this terrorist business right from the beginning.

CHAPTER THREE

FBI agent Donald Peterson was worried. He was harassed, tormented and worried. Now someone who claimed official connections had talked his way through the local police, airport police, and FBI cordon, and wanted to see him. All this, while a planeload of passengers was speeding toward the airport under control of machine-gun-wielding members of the Black Liberation Front.

It was not bad enough that the reporters and the television cameramen had to be kept at bay or that the legions of the curious were growing and threatening to almost guarantee casualties if shooting broke out. But some man without any identification was tugging at Peterson's sleeve and the guards seemed unable to budge him. Three guards, one man, and he stood right in the control tower as if his feet were cemented to the floor—and he had the awesome nerve to tell agent Peterson to phone his own headquarters.

"Mister," said Peterson, spinning angrily around, "you get out of this control tower right now or you're under arrest for obstructing justice."

"And you'll be stationed in Anchorage," answered the man coldly. "That plane was rerouted to this airport so that I, personally, could go on board and deliver the ransom."

Well, didn't that beat it all? That was the capper. Peterson had been called suddenly from Chicago to take command of the airport in a Situation Blue—hijacking, political—and now this stranger knew more about it than he did. Peterson was sure of that. The airplane actually had no business in Los Angeles. It had been an East Coast flight and there had been dozens of airports where it could have landed.

So just before starting from Chicago, he had asked headquarters why Los Angeles had been chosen as the payoff site, and indeed, why they were paying off at all when the latest national policy was not to pay off. "I thought the policy was to hang tough," Peterson had told his superior's telephone voice.

"The policy is for you to go to the airport. The money will be ready there."

Orders, as always, had been orders. A military fighter had sped Peterson to L.A. and as soon as he had started setting up his men and arranging the airport for emergency action, the crowds began to form. The reporters, with that special news sense, began breaking police lines and before he knew it, the radio was announcing that the plane was headed for Los Angeles.

"Call headquarters," said the man without identification.

Peterson looked at the man, estimating him. His eyes were cold and still, with a strange, vague Oriental quality, a deadly coldness Peterson had seen only once, long before, when he had witnessed an execution in Korea. But this man was white.

"What's your name?" Peterson asked.

"Remo."

"Mr. Remo, who are you with and what's your business here?"

"Remo's my first name and you have instructions

36

concerning me. I'm sorry they haven't gotten through yet."

"All right," said Peterson. "I'll tell you what I'm going to do. I'm going to phone my headquarters. And if there is no instruction concerning you, you are under arrest. And if you resist arrest, I'm going to shoot you dead."

"Make the phone call. And when you're through, get those snipers out of the hangar entrance. They're too obvious. They may get someone killed and I don't want any stray bullets flying. I don't like sloppiness."

The snipers were four hundred yards away and hidden by tarpaulin. Remo had seen the tarpaulin flap—but in a direction against the wind. He saw the surprise on Peterson's face that anyone had noticed his concealed snipers from such a distance.

Peterson signalled for a telephone. He stood before the banks of darkened radar screens and dialed, looking at Remo, then glancing down at the screen on the far left. He was a handsome man, with a strong, black face that was now taut with frustration.

"That our blip?" asked Remo.

Peterson refused to answer.

Remo felt a guard tighten his grip on a bicep. While looking at Peterson, Remo expanded the muscle, filling it with constant pressure as he had been taught, then suddenly, like a balloon being punctured, releasing the pressure. He didn't look at the guard but he felt the hand searching around warily for the muscle, and for a few moments as he watched Peterson's face tighten, he played hide and seek with the guard, weaving the bicep full, then relaxing it, then expanding the

37

tricep, then contracting it, so the guard felt as if he had a sleeveful of hard hamsters in his grip.

"Are you sure?" said Peterson into the phone. "Would you repeat that? Yes. Yes. Yes. But with what department . . . ? Yes, sir." Peterson hung up the phone and sighed. He turned to Remo.

"All right. Do you have any suggestions? Or orders?"

The guards, knowing whence power flowed, released their hold on Remo.

"No," Remo said. "Nothing much. Keep everyone out of the way. Give me the money in sacks and I'll go on board and talk to the hijackers."

"But how about the passengers? We should negotiate for their release."

"Worry, worry, worry. Why are you worried?" Remo said.

"A lot of people could get killed," said Peterson angrily.

"So," said Remo.

"That would be a disaster," said Peterson. "If a lot of people get killed. That is a bad thing. That is a very bad thing whether you know it or not."

"Could be worse," said Remo.

"Yeah? How?"

"We could be incompetent, that's worse. You have no control over fate, but you do have control over your competence."

"Jeezus. They really send them all to me," growled Peterson, shaking his head.

Peterson was instructed to get all snipers away from the runways. Remo, the money and Peterson would wait at the end of the runway the hijacked plane was to

38

land on. Remo would deliver the cash. It was waiting for them in two white canvas sacks in the back of an armored car.

"Did you want to keep the incident from the press for the time being?" Remo asked.

Peterson nodded.

"Having an armored car come to the airport isn't the way to do it."

"So that's how the newsboys found out. Well, we'll know better next time."

"You planning on institutionalizing hijacking?" Remo said.

As they waited on the runway, Peterson and Remo in a closed car with the two sacks on the hood of the car so the hijackers could see it from the plane windows, Peterson outlined the problems.

"This is no ordinary group of hijackers. We don't know their destination yet. And, get a load of this, they have a .50 caliber machine gun aboard. We believe it is mounted at the entrance to the cockpit, controlling the seats. A .50 caliber machine gun."

"It will make a nice earring," said Remo, gazing out into the darkening sky, watching the flight of a gull dip and pivot and then make its way off toward the Pacific, where gulls belonged.

"They got that gun through our latest detection devices. Our latest. The goddam thing will find gold fillings in your teeth, and they got it past that. That's like moving an elephant through a turnstile with no one seeing you do it."

"Elephant?" said Remo.

"Yes. A comparison," said Peterson.

"Oh," said Remo.

"I don't think you're going to get out of this thing alive," said Peterson.

"I'll get out alive," said Remo. He looked for the gull, but it had disappeared into the vast nothing that was the sky.

"Pretty sure of yourself, aren't you?" said Peterson.

"When you tie your shoelaces, do you worry about breaking your thumbs?"

"You're that confident."

"Pretty much," said Remo. "Tell me about this machine gun. Is it really so extraordinary to get it through your detection gadget?"

"Up till now, I would have said impossible. This is a whole new bag of worms."

Remo nodded. So that was why Smith had begun to pull out all the CURE stops, use all the CURE influence, and get him here to meet the plane. Smith was sure that this group was part of the new terrorist wave he was worked up about.

Smith had lectured for a full afternoon, explaining how these terrorists with their new techniques could make international sanctions look like so much wallpaper. *Instant competence,* he had called it.

"You know something I don't know?" Peterson asked.

Remo nodded.

"You with the CIA?"

"No," said Remo.

"Aeronautics?"

"No."

"Pentagon?"

Remo shook his head.

"Who are you with?"

"The Insurance Association of America. Do you know that if 800,000 people were killed instantly, insurance stocks would drop almost a point on the Dow Jones? Horrifying, isn't it?"

"You're a wise sonofabitch," said Peterson, "and I hope they get you."

Remo squinted into the horizon.

"That's our baby, I think."

"Where?"

Remo pointed northward.

"I don't see anything."

"Wait."

Five minutes elapsed before Peterson could make out a faint dot in the sky.

"Do you have binoculars in your skull?"

"We in the insurance industry have to. . . ."

"Oh, shut up."

The plane came in on a single line approach. No circling. There was no need. Traffic had been cleared in the area. Remo watched the giant silver machine set down like a house being lowered, slowly, and then it was on the runway far away and coming toward them. He could see the twirl of propellers. The plane halted in a cough of dying engines. Remo heard fumbling and banging at the main plane door. The hijackers could commandeer a plane but they didn't know how to open a door. Yet, they knew how to smuggle a machine gun on board. They were also, undoubtedly, weapons wise. No matter.

The door flew open and a large man in dashiki and Afro stood in the doorway, a Kalishnikov cradled in his right hand, a megaphone in his left. Add personal weapons to the .50 caliber. All of them past the new perfect

41

security system. Maybe they even had an elephant on board.

"You there in the car. Come out with your hands in front of you. Open the doors and trunk so we can see inside," came the booming voice from the megaphone.

Not bad, thought Remo. They were careful. He nodded to Peterson, who opened the doors.

"I don't have a key to the trunk," Peterson yelled up to the plane.

"Shoot it open," said the man in the plane doorway. Very clever. A check to see if Peterson was armed.

"I don't have a gun," Peterson said.

"Well, throw up the money."

Remo hopped out of the car and grabbed the two satchels of cash sitting on the hood. He held them in front of him.

"I will bring up the money. But I want the passengers released. Now, I don't expect you to release the passengers before I give you the money but I do expect the passengers to walk out. So let my friend here drive the car away and get a boarding platform to the plane so the people can walk off after I give you the money."

"No. The money now or we kill a hostage."

"If you kill a hostage, not one of you will leave that plane alive," yelled Remo. "Think about it. You open fire on one hostage and we go for broke."

"We are ready to die and live in Paradise for Allah."

"Feel free," said Remo.

"Ah could shoot, you know."

"If I go, everyone goes."

"You lying."

"Try me."

42

"Ah knows your evil ways."

"Feel free to try me."

"Jess a minute."

The black head disappeared into the plane. All right, he wasn't the leader. His head returned and it said:

"Okay, but if you try any funny stuff, a hostage will die and the death will be on your hands."

"That's mighty white of you," Remo said. He watched his opponent blanch. Good. A little unnerving never did an opponent any good. He held the Kalishnikov with skill, finger ready at the trigger, but not on it.

Peterson looked to Remo.

"Get the car out and a platform in," said Remo, keeping his back to the air terminal. The photographers must be blazing away and who knew who had a telephoto lens. Maybe they had a good shot of his face already.

As the boarding platform made its slow way to the plane, Remo chatted with the man at the plane door.

"Have a nice flight?" he asked.

"Our flight to freedom will be the greatest flight."

"I mean the food. First class or tourist?"

"When you pack weapons, you always travel first class," said the man with the Afro.

"How true," Remo said. "How true."

As the ramp eased to the plane door, Remo watched the trigger finger move closer to the trigger. The barrel raised to just about the line where men might be hidden on the steps. The ramp touched, the black man stepped out onto the platform, Kalishnikov at the ready, and peered down. He nodded then for Remo to come on board. Like a passenger bound for a week's vaca-

43

tion, Remo gingerly boarded the plane with the two sacks of money.

"I brought a little something as a plane-warming gift," Remo said.

"Cool, man," said the gunman. "Just carry those sacks to the front of the plane."

Heads turned to look at Remo, frightened faces, men and women, black and white, children and grown-ups, joined now by their common fear. At the pilot's cockpit was what Agent Peterson had predicted. A mounted .50 caliber machine gun.

The fear in the old prop airplane was palpable. He could smell it. It was a mix of adrenalin, perspiration, released urine—a combination of odors.

"Heads forward," commanded a black woman in yellow dashiki and high turban. The passengers looked forward. Remo walked up the aisle directly to the muzzle of the .50 caliber. It was pointed at his groin.

A man squatted behind the gun and the woman stood over him.

"Put down the bags," she ordered.

Remo lowered the bags.

"Close the door, Kareem," she yelled to the guard at the rear of the plane.

"Just a minute," said Remo. "You don't need these hostages."

The woman looked coldly at Remo. Her face was fatty but hard and her neck rolled in darkening thickness.

"Don't tell me what I need and don't need."

"You don't need seventy frightened people who might do something stupid. Not when you've got me and the pilot and the co-pilot."

"And the stewardesses," she said. Her voice was clipped and her accent was Boston or New England.

"You don't need the stewardesses either. A hostage is a hostage. Anything more than that is baggage."

"You're very concerned with my problems," she said.

"I'd like to see the passengers and stewardesses out of a tense situation. I'm showing you why it's in your interest also."

The woman pondered a moment and Remo could see the quick sharp calculations begin in her eyes.

"Open the bags," she said.

Remo unsnapped both canvas bags and brought out two hands full of money. "Small unmarked bills," he said.

"Put them back. You're not as good a hostage as seventy people."

"I think so. I'm vice president of the First Trust Company of Los Angeles," said Remo nodding to the markers on the canvas bags. "You know what we capitalists think of bankers."

A cold smile crossed the woman's face.

"You don't look like a banker."

"You don't look like a terrorist."

"You'll be the first to die if anything goes wrong," she said and then, waving to the back of the plane, barked an order. "Kareem, open the door."

She did not announce to the passengers that they would be freed, but told the rows closest to her to stand, then waved them to the rear of the plane. Shrewd enough to avoid panic, Remo thought. The plane emptied in less than three minutes. A young black boy wanted to return to his seat to get his toy fire engine, but his mother tugged him along angrily.

"Let him take his engine," said the woman in the dashiki.

One of the stewardesses refused to leave. "I'm not leaving until the pilots leave," she said.

"You're leaving," said the woman in dashiki, then Kareem grabbed the pale neck and flung her down the aisle and out the door. He shut it behind her.

The woman knocked on the cabin door. It opened, and a small black man with a large forehead and metal-rimmed eyeglasses poked his head out. Remo saw the tip of a .357 Magnum.

"You people wouldn't happen to have any elephants on board this thing, would you?" said Remo.

"Who is that?" asked the man with the Magnum.

"A banker. Our hostage. We have the money. We can go now. How is fuel?"

"Fuel's adequate," said the pistol-wielder.

"Okay, let's move it," said the woman.

The engines revved up and Remo felt the plane gather power for the takeoff.

"Do I stand here or may I sit?"

"Stand," said the woman.

"If the plane jerks, I could lose my balls."

"We're willing to take that risk."

"If you're willing to parachute with your bodies, why should you care about mine, right?" asked Remo.

The woman's face remained cold. "What makes you think we're going to parachute?"

"Your fuel. This is a prop job. You would have grabbed a jet if you were going out of the country. So you're going back east, I guess. The plane wouldn't go too far. Just for guesses, I'd say you're headed for some-where mid-American, cause that's a good middle point,

46

and for the sake of a good parachute escape, I'd say some very desolate or woody place where you're not going to land on Main Street."

"You're not a banker, are you?" asked the woman. Remo shrugged.

"I hope you'll do as a hostage. For your sake," she said.

"You're pretty arrogant for a corpse," said Remo and when the plane reached four thousand feet, he smiled at the machine gunner.

"Guess what?" he said.

"What?" said the machiner gunner.

"You lose," said Remo and came down with his pinkies, shattering the machine gunner's wrists. The black head came forward and Remo clapped flat hands against eardrums, creating skull pressure like a concussion grenade. The eyes bulged and were blank in death.

It happened so quickly, the dashiki-clad woman barely got a hand on a pistol inside her garment. Remo squeezed the wrist and hoisted her, hand under butt like a bag of groceries, and used her as a chest-high shield as he dashed down toward the rear of the plane where Kareem was trying to get a clear shot. Instead, he got the woman, full face, bodies colliding with a whoomph against the lavatory door.

Up front the cockpit door opened and Remo snatched his human shield again for another run. This time, he did not hurl her hefty unconscious body into the gunman, but moved forward around her just as he reached the cockpit door. A downward hand chop and the pistol fell harmlessly to the carpeted aisle, and the man tumbled over the dead machine gunner. The barrel of the .50 caliber pointed harmlessly to the ceiling.

"You guys okay in there?" Remo yelled into the cockpit.

"Yeah, what happened?" said the pilot turning around.

Remo moved his face away from the door so the pilot could not see him. "Nothing," he said. "The plane is secured."

"We can head back to L.A. then?"

"Not yet. Better give me ten minutes of air-time, and then head back. I've got some talking to do. And stay off the radio for a few minutes." Remo reached over the two male bodies and shut the cabin door.

He hauled the dashiki-clad woman and the pistol-wielder down the aisle, like baggage, to Kareem, who was regaining consciousness. With cups of water splashed on them, they all woke up. The pistol-wielder groaned when he tried to move his right hand.

"Wha happened?" said Kareem.

The three hijackers sat, rump on aisle, back to lavatory door.

"We're going to play a game," said Remo. "It's called Truth or Consequences. I ask you questions and you answer them right or you pay the consequences."

"I demand a lawyer. I know my constitutional rights," snapped the dashiki-clad woman.

"Well, there's a little problem with that," Remo said. "Because of people like you, our government has an agency that works outside the Constitution. This agency employs one of the meanest sons of bitches you are ever going to meet. He wasn't trained in legal technicalities. In fact, he only follows the law of the jungle."

"And that's you, honkie, right?" said the woman.

"Well, let me warn you, you try any of your police brutality and they'll be a picket line from here to Washington looking for your ass. You hear me, honkie. Looking for your ass."

Remo smiled and with a fluid move of his right hand, shattered her raised kneecap.

"Aaargh," screamed the woman, grabbing for her knee.

"That's my introduction. I'm the mean son of a bitch. Now for your names, folks. Believe me. After this, you'll welcome police brutality."

"Kahlala Waled," said the woman, her face screwed in pain.

"Your real name."

"That is my real name."

"You've got another knee."

"Leronia Smith."

"All right. Good. Now you, Kareem."

"Tyrone Jackson."

"And you?" said Remo to the man who had held the cockpit.

"Mustafa El Faquar."

"Let's try again," said Remo.

"Mustafa El Faquar."

"No. Not the game of the guy who sold your great grandpa to the slave traders. Your name."

"Mustafa El Faquar."

Remo shrugged. So be it. He caught the man by the fold in his neck and hoisting him off his backside dragged him the two steps to the door. With his left hand, he snapped open the plane door. A wind gust slapped his face. The pistol-wielder's dashiki fluttered like a flag amok.

"Okay, Mustafa. Why don't you think about it on the way to the street?"

"You wouldn't throw me out. You full of shit."

"What do I have to do," Remo said, "to convince you people I'm not your friendly police community relations team?"

"You bluffing, whitey."

"Goodbye, sweetheart," said Remo and flipped the neck into the wind. The body followed and disappered without even the scream catching up to the open door.

Kahlala Waled and Kareem suddenly realized they had not been oppressed for three hundred years, and began to think of Remo as a friend. Really a friend. They hadn't even wanted to do the hijacking. They were just led astray.

"Thass right, astray," said Tyrone Jackson, alias Kareem.

Who led them astray?

A radical. A real rotten mother. Did they wish they had him here now. Would they tell him a thing or two. Kahlala and Kareem loved America. Loved people of all races. Loved mankind. Martin Luther King had the right idea.

"You're right," Remo said. "I could never handle a Martin Luther King. But you two are right up my alley. Now what is the name of your leader and where did you get your training?"

They didn't know his name, but the training was at Patton College, near Seneca Falls, New York.

"Come on now, who trained you?"

"We never saw him. Honest," said Tyrone.

Remo believed him. He believed Tyrone because those were the last words on Tyrone's lips all the way to the door and through it.

"All right, ma'am," said Remo. "Give me a fast rundown on your training, how many months, what methods."

"An afternoon," said the woman. Her eyes were tearing from the pain in her knee.

"Let me pay you a compliment. You're too good for an afternoon. Too damned good. Now, let's try again."

"I swear. An afternoon. You're not going to kill me, are you?"

"Of course I am," said Remo.

"Then you go screw, you honkie bastard."

Remo said goodbye to the woman and ushered her to the door, shutting it behind her wind-whipped robes. She had vanished into a cloud, when Remo snapped his fingers in annoyance. Damn. He had forgotten to ask them. How had they smuggled the weapons aboard the plane? Smith would be sure to ask him that. Damn and double damn.

Remo went to the cockpit and told the pilot to return to Los Angeles. At the airport, a team of radical lawyers were waiting for their clients. Remo told Agent Peterson, the first man to board the plane, that the lawyers should have left their briefcases at home and brought sponges instead. The parachutists tried to escape, he explained, and their chutes failed to open. Remo vanished into the crowd, and the next day, when Peterson told a superior that a man from Washington headquarters had killed the hijackers, he was brought up on quiet departmental charges. Washington, an agency spokesman said, had never sent any such man. Peterson would face a departmental hearing. Privately, he was assured that he would face nothing worse than ten years in Anchorage.

CHAPTER FOUR

Remo turned the Rolls off the Palisades Parkway onto the New York Thruway. He had driven from the coast nonstop and nonsleep, the last thousand miles of which were accompanied by Chiun's complaints. They ceased only when the daytime serials began. Chiun sat in the back seat with his portable television rig. With Remo's driving up front, it made it seem as if he were now the chauffeur for the Master of Sinanju. The problem was Barbra Streisand.

When Chiun had heard Seneca Falls was in New York State, he had asked:

"Is that near Brooklyn?"

"No, it's not near Brooklyn."

"But it is in the same province."

"At opposite ends."

"We will pass Brooklyn on our way to Seneca Falls, correct?"

"Not exactly. It's out of our way."

"A little stop in Brooklyn would not be so awesome a task for a 'not-exactly.' "

"What's in Brooklyn, Chiun?" Remo had asked.

"I wish to visit the monument to Barbra Streisand who was born there."

"I don't think there is a monument in Brooklyn to Barbra Streisand."

Chiun looked up, puzzled.

"You have a Washington Monument, correct?"

"Yeah," said Remo.

"And a Lincoln Memorial?"

"Yeah."

"You have a Columbus Circle?"

"Yeah."

"Then let us visit the Streisand monument, for surely if Americans could honor a lecher, a failure and a navigator who got lost, they must mark the birthplace of one of their most beautiful souls."

"Chiun. Barbra Streisand is not a national hero."

"And that is the sort of country you think worth saving?" asked Chiun. He had been silent since Youngstown, Ohio, when "As the Planet Revolves" came on. Remo could have sworn that the plot never changed, not even the point in the plot that he had overheard the year before in Miami when Dr. Ramsey Duncan feared telling Rebecca Wentworth that her stepfather, William Vogelman, the discoverer of a cure for malnutrition among the Auca Indians, was not her stepfather at all but the lover of her half-sister who had threatened suicide. Zipping out of Youngstown one year later, Remo heard the television set in the back seat disclose that Dr. Duncan was still pondering whether to tell Rebecca about her stepfather.

But now, in New York State, the soap operas were ended and Chiun was sitting silently in the back seat, his eyes closed.

Dr. Smith had wanted Remo to fly to Patton College, but Remo feared being seen at any airport. The news was full of the mystery-man imposter who had boarded the plane and perhaps even pushed them to their deaths, and while the cameras only got the back of Remo's head, and the artist's sketches were no closer to his looks than the cover of a paperback book, all airports were very much aware of a six-foot man with dark eyes and thick wrists.

Smith had continued his strange excitability concerning this terrorist thing—Dr. Harold W. Smith, who had been chosen a decade or more before to head CURE because of his integrity and stability.

Smith had flown out to Los Angeles to brief Remo personally again, knowing full well that each meeting was a risk to CURE's almost sacred cover.

"We can get you to Patton College tonight. Navy Phantom. Less than three hours from coast to coast," Smith had said.

"With the whole country associating air and the mystery man? Suppose someone gets word of a guy looking like me getting taken for a ride in a Navy jet? C'mon, Smitty. What's the matter with you?"

"You don't know how urgent this is, Remo."

"All the more reason to be careful and proper and competent."

"You're beginning to sound like Chiun now," Smith said.

"I'm beginning to sound like you used to sound."

"You've got to smash them now, Remo. Now."

"I'll get them, and I'll get them right. Now relax."

"The international conference on terrorism is scheduled for New York next week. We can't allow this force to be in existence by then. Do you understand? Do you really understand what's involved?"

"Yes," said Remo. "We're up against it."

"Right," said Smith, and suddenly his lemon face flushed maroon.

"Are you all right?" Remo asked softly.

"Yes, yes. I'm fine. Fine. Perfectly all right."

"Can I get you a glass of water?"

"No. I'm all right."

That had been two days and a few thousand miles ago and Remo was still worried about Smith, not that he cared really about the man's well-being. Rather, Smith uncorked was like a violation of the universe as Remo knew it. Smith knew what the job could do to him, and Remo knew what his own waiting due-bill was. Still, to see Smith like that, well. . . .

Remo slowed the Rolls to pick up an entrance ticket at the toll booth. The late afternoon sun cast a reddish glow over the foothills around them. Only the smoggy pollution of the air reminded Remo they were still near a major city.

"We have passed Brooklyn," said Chiun as Remo sped into the center lane.

"Yes."

"It would have been nice to see the street where she was born."

"Streisand?"

"Yes. It would have been a blessed relief for a poor aging benefactor who has given so much to so unworthy a recipient."

"Well, we're not going back to Brooklyn, Chiun."

"I know," said Chiun sadly. "I know that Brooklyn would be out of your way. It would be an inconvenience. And who am I to cause you any inconvenience, no matter how my heart longs for a bit of pleasure? After all, I am only the man who has transformed worthless cow dung into. . . ."

"Yes," said Remo, attentive now, awaiting praise.

". . . into something barely adequate," said Chiun. "In this world, there is no reward for excellence, for

56

perfection. What a man gives, he gives, and from the ungrateful it never comes back."

"We're not going to Brooklyn, Chiun."

"I know that, Remo. Because I know you."

On that, Remo knew he must avoid getting close to other cars. When piqued, Chiun had a habit of taking vengeance on passing vehicles. His long nailed hands would flick out the car window and snip an aerial or a rear view mirror off a passing car. Then Chiun would smile and wave at the driver.

Remo felt the wind at the back of his neck and knew Chiun was readying his game. Remo managed to save a Volkwagen and a Buick but failed on a beige Cadillac Brougham whose driver waved back pleasantly with a smile. This robbed Chiun of his pleasure and Remo felt the wind cease on his neck. The window was up.

"Little Father," said Remo seriously, "I am worried. I am worried about Smith."

"It is a good thing to put one's mind to the well-being of an employer. But not to worry. To understand."

"I think Smith is losing his balance and I don't know what to do about it."

"The only thing you can do, my son. Your craft, taught to you as it was taught to me. Practice your calling."

"But. . . ."

"But *this* and but *that*. There is always a but to excuse a foolish move. You have one thing that you do better than any white man. You are not skilled in diplomacy or the civil service, nor can you lead hundreds of men. You are an assassin. Be satisfied with that. For if you fail in that, you fail in all things."

"I just wish I could do something, dammit."

"And I wish I could be a sparrow," said Chium.

"Why a sparrow?"

"So I could fly from here and visit Brooklyn before the ends of my days."

"You never let up, do you, Chiun? Never. All right. I promise you, when this thing is over, we will visit Brooklyn and find the house where Barbra Streisand was born. Okay? Okay? Does that satisfy you?"

"We could turn around now," said Chiun, "and get it over with so you would not have anything on your mind."

"I give up," said Remo.

"Then we are turning around?"

"No," said Remo.

"You give up in the most peculiar of ways," said the Master of Sinanju, and, having been denied a promised pledge, said not another word until the car reached the outskirts of Seneca Falls in the middle of the night.

CHAPTER FIVE

Remo expected little difficulty in finding the training site, at or near Patton College.

A training site had certain requirements you couldn't fit in a one-room apartment. The Kalishnikov rifles the hijackers had used, for example. If you were going to fire them at something other than point blank range, you needed a minimum of fifty feet and an optimum minimum of one hundred feet. Ideally, a good range would be fifty yards.

You also had to fire it into something other than a blackboard.

For a terrorist, nerves were needed. The most common training was fire—going through it. Fires left scorches.

Obstacle courses and plane mockups were also useful. In short, if there was any training going on, Remo would find the place.

After recovering from his shock that Remo had failed to find out how the weapons were smuggled past the metal detector, Smith had warned him that the terrorists' training might be unlike any training that military minds were aware of.

"Then they'll leave traces unlike those from any other training. Relax, Smitty. They're dead meat. Okay?"

It was a small campus and Remo strolled it alone. Chiun claimed he was exhausted from the trip, but Remo knew if Chiun had thought there would be anything of interest on an American college campus, he could have stayed awake a week if he wished. It was no magic trick, just an ability to sleep in shorter periods more continuously, the use of odd seconds instead of hours.

Naturally Patton College had a Fayerweather Hall. Every campus seemed to have one. The administration building was little more than a shack but the main buildings rose brick and aluminum modern, forming squares around large green lawns.

Remo was sure training wouldn't be on the lawns but he strolled them anyway. Not a divot. A few of the coeds eyed him and he smiled back, not an encouraging smile but a recognition of their interest. He would have liked to have gone to a college like this and when he had been a living person with an identity, a patrolman on the Newark Police Force, he had enrolled in an extension school at Rutgers. He couldn't afford to go to a school like this in the daytime. If he had, who knew, maybe he never would have been recruited by CURE and maybe he would have a wife and family by now.

He knew, however, that the attractiveness of a family existed only because he didn't have to endure one. Still, it would be nice to know that children would carry on the name. Hell, he didn't even have one, other than his first name, and being an orphan, he wasn't all that sure that either name—Remo or Williams—really belonged to him.

He wandered into the gym. A gym would be an ideal place. A man with a pot belly and a whistle stood on the side watching about fifty, mostly beefy athletes, go through set exercises. He was in his late forties and wore a baseball cap. He had to be a coach. No middle-aged man other than a coach would wear a baseball cap, unless, of course, he was an admiral, and Patton College was landlocked.

"Spring practice?" asked Remo.

"Yeah," grunted the coach. "Who're you?"

"Freelance writer doing a round-up on small colleges. Their use of gymnasiums and things like that."

"Hey, you," screamed the coach. "Move your fucking ass, you lazy cunt." He waved a clipboard at a young man who, Remo could tell instantly, was working incorrectly on a damaged knee.

"We like to use our gym," the coach said softly to Remo, "to build character. That's the whole philosophy of Patton athletics. Hey, you, Johnson. You do those pushups clean or it's back to the ghetto. You're not in Harlem, anymore."

The coach took a brief moment to deny there was any racial friction on the team and he wanted Remo to print that. "We've got good boys here. Good boys."

Was the gym used twenty-four hours a day?

The coach shook his head.

Was there a rifle team?

Nah.

Martial arts classes?

"Nahhh, that's faggy. Give a guy a shot in the head and that's it. You know, pow, in the head. With the fist. American. I don't go for that gook stuff. Don't print that, though. You can say we view the athletic field as a laboratory for building understanding. Hey, you, Ginsberg. You waiting for your mother to make that pushup? Let's get into it. Petrolli! Get the grease out of your ass. . . . Athletics, as you may know, constitutes an extension of the Greek philosophy of sound

61

body and sound mind. It's not whether you win or lose, it's how you play the game."

"Have a losing season last year?"

"Well, let me explain that. You see, we really didn't lose if you look at the statistics." Remo examined the walls as the coach went into a statistical explanation that would do justice to the wildest fantasies of a government economist. "So you see, on the whole, we've really had a winning season."

"Yeah," said Remo. "Say if you should see an old Oriental guy anywhere in long flowing robes, don't mention things like gook. Okay?"

"Hell, what do you take me for? I know how to handle gooks. There was one here last week. I talked to him just like everybody else."

"Mighty white of you. Was he Korean, Chinese, Vietnamese, Japanese? What?"

"A gook."

"Well, now that you've got it down to a billion people."

"A gook's a gook."

"I hope you never find out the difference. I hate to clean up bodies."

The janitor, for twenty dollars, confirmed that there was no rifle range, no explosions, no fires, no karate classes. Radical movements? Some. Did they meet anyplace special? No.

The basements of the dormitories showed nothing, nor did the chemistry labs or the physics building, the Student Union, or even the banks of Cayuga Lake or the old barge canal which bordered two sides of the campus.

They had to train somewhere. You don't put people

on airplanes with rifles without training, and you definitely don't sneak .50 caliber machine guns past metal detectors without planning. And if this group was, as Smith suspected, part of the new wave of terrorists, they definitely had to have large amounts of space to create terrorist squads and guerilla armies. Not that that was done here in the halls of Patton, but if the training techniques were similar, there had to be plenty of useable space.

Remo wandered back into the Student Union, glancing at the menu in the cafeteria. Enough starch content to stiffen the living. He took a glass of water and sat down in a booth near some students who, like many youngsters and older lunatics, had solutions to problems of the world. Invariably these solutions required levels of mass morality that would shame a saint. These levels of morality, to be immediately adopted by mankind, were usually introduced by words such as "merely" or "just," such as "If only the police would just stop looking at brick throwers as enemies," or, "If everyone would merely stop thinking of their own self-interest," and, "Blacks just have to get together and think as one."

Remo sipped the water. The youngsters in the next booth had narrowed the solutions to man's problems down to one. "Merely have everyone think of himself as part of one world family." The methods for achieving this world salvation somehow included, as its initial action, emptying garbage cans at Fayerweather Hall.

Remo closed his eyes for a moment. Had he been wrong about Patton College? Had the three skyjackers lied? He thought back to the plane, and tried to rebuild the scene in his mind. Seventy persons, terrified hostages. Four skyjackers, all with weapons. In his mind, he looked around the plane's cabin. Nothing. Rows of seats. An old wheelchair propped against the wall in the back. Stewardesses looking tired and tweety. But he should have found out how they got the weapons aboard. And he should have found out why the plane had gone on to L.A. Sure, Smith wanted Remo to deliver the money. But the hijackers had control of that. If they had told the pilot, land here or get your brains blown out, he would have landed. Why had they agreed to L.A.? It was almost as if it had been part of their plan. But why? He should have asked. He should have asked a lot of things. But he was sure of one thing. They had not lied about Patton College. Fear was the greatest truth serum of them all. So where the hell was the training site? Remo let his mind wander and as he did, universal peace seemed easier. Maybe he could start it by throwing an egg at the dean of women or something. Then he felt the vibrations of someone sitting down.

"Bastards. The bastards," said a young girl.

Remo opened his eyes. A pert-faced girl surrounded by a strong shag cut of blonde hair was sitting across the table. She was crying.

"The bastards."

"What's the matter?"

"The bastards. They won't let me get a word in edgewise."

"That's too bad," said Remo without enthusiasm.

"They never let me say anything. Especially when I have something good. Robert and Carol and Theodore always do all the talking and I never get a chance. I had something very good. Excellent. But no one would let me say it. They just didn't ask if I had something and they could see, if they looked close, that I had something to say."

"Oh," said Remo.

"Yes," said the girl, taking a paper napkin from a metal holder on the table between her and Remo. "I had a wonderful plan. All you have to do for a revolution is to kill the millionaires and the policemen. Without policemen, there'd be no police brutality. Without millionaires, there'd be no capitalism."

"Uh, who's going to do all this killing?"

"The people," said the girl.

"I see. Anyone in particular?"

"You know, the people," said the girl, as if everyone knew who the people were. "Blacks and poor."

"Just in America?"

"No. The Third World throughout."

"I see. And what will you be doing?"

"I'll help lead it, but I'll step aside for Third World leadership. I'll be the catalyst to help bring it about."

"What if *they* don't let you get a word in edgewise?"

"Oh, no. Third World people are nice. They're not like Robert or Carol or Theodore."

"You think a Zulu chief is going to let you outline his future for him?"

"The tribal chiefs of Africa are only a remnant of neo-colonial exploitation and we'll have to remove them too."

"I see. What, if anything, do you learn here at Patton?"

"History and political science. But it's really irrelevant. I just cram for the exams to get an establishment piece of paper that says I'm legally allowed to teach.

I mean, the paper won't make me any better a teacher. But you know the establishment."

Remo toyed with the water glass.

"You're probably very proud of the hijackers . . . the revolutionaries who were killed recently."

"Are you part of it?" asked the girl, her button brown eyes widening in excitement.

Remo winked.

"Gee, I didn't think anybody hardly knew they came from here. I mean, they weren't students. You're not a cop, are you?"

"Do I look like a cop?" said former Patrolman Remo Williams.

"Gee, I don't know, man, you could be. I mean, your hair isn't long or anything."

Remo suddenly became very interested in the girl as a person. He asked her name. It was Joan. Joan Hacker, but Remo said that was the wrong name. She was starlight. She was truly starlight. Joan thought that was corny. Remo touched her arm and smiled. She thought Remo had a nice smile, but he could still be a cop. He smiled and listened. Starlight's father was a chemical engineer. He was a male chauvinist pig oppressor who revoked her American Express card and went pigging around, begging for approval and gratitude, just because he footed the bill for this bourgeois irrelevant institution. Starlight's mother was an unliberated woman who refused to be liberated no matter how hard Starlight tried.

Starlight's roommate was a nosy, aloof bitch who did nothing but paint her body to be attractive to male chauvinist pigs. Starlight's professors, except for her sociology teacher, were backward bourgeois nincom-

66

poops. Her sociology teacher had given her an A because of her term paper on how to conduct a successful revolution. Starlight's greatest ambition was to fight for the Viet Cong but since her father had revoked her American Express card, she couldn't afford the airfare.

Starlight was for all oppressed people and against oppressors. Starlight's bust was a 38-D. Did Remo know that Starlight had taken the pill since she was sixteen?

Starlight was outlining what America and the world really needed, later that afternoon in her dormitory room, when Remo gave her what she needed. Three times.

Remo pressed her young nude body to him and waited for an expression of gratitude. Instead, he felt her hand run to reactivate the pleasure maker. She wanted more. She got more. Two more.

"You really know how to get things started," said Starlight.

"Started?" said Remo.

"You're going to stop?" asked Starlight.

"No," said Remo and by nightfall, Starlight finally believed he was not a policeman. She lay cuddled in his arms, kissing his shoulder.

"I believe in the revolution," Remo whispered in her ear.

"Do you? Do you really?"

"Yes," said Remo. "I think the heroes who died in the airplane to free oppressed people are Patton's greatest contribution to civilization."

"They really weren't matriculated," said Joan Hacker. "One took night school courses and the others weren't students."

67

"Go on," said Remo, in amazement. "You didn't know *them?*"

"I did, too. I supplied the coffee and food. I paid for the lunch."

"The lunch?"

"Sure. It came out of my allowance but I considered it an honor. I suffered for the revolution."

"They had only one lunch?"

"How many lunches can you eat in one day?"

Remo sat up in bed. "They trained somewhere else and spent one day here, right?"

Joan Hacker shook her head and reached up for Remo to return his body to hers.

"Answer my question first," said Remo.

"No. They trained in the afternoon, after lunch, and they left that night. Me and a bunch of other students who are liberated served the food and sort of stood guard. We didn't hear what was going on but it was very exciting. And then we heard what they had done."

"Where did you stand guard?"

"By the barge canal. None of us even saw the instructor. We didn't know what they were going to do. But yesterday when all those people came asking questions, we knew it had been traced back here. What's the matter? I felt your shoulders tighten."

"Nothing," said Remo. "Nothing. I'm just overcome by the revolutionary ardor you show."

Remo was overcome all right. By a gnawing suspicion about Smith.

"These people asking questions. Were they police? FBI?"

Joan Hacker shook her head. "Funny kind of people. None of them said they were police. Are you all right?"

"Sure, sure," said Remo. Well, they were CURE people, elements from the vast network who didn't know who they really worked for. Smith hadn't been able to wait. He couldn't wait for the two days it would take Remo to drive cross country. Remo remembered Chiun's admonition, not to worry about Smith, but to continue plying his trade. He also remembered that Chiun had answers to things that stumped western minds. He would ask the Master of Sinanju how a person could be trained in just one afternoon. He would take him to the spot near the river that Joan Hacker had described, and ask Chiun, what had gone on here? And Remo would be shocked by the answer.

"You sure you're all right?" Joan asked again. "Maybe you'd like a little snort?" She pointed to a little metal cannister on her end table.

"No," Remo said. "But don't let me stop you. Go ahead and enjoy yourself."

"Thanks," she said. "I will. After all this, I think a little coke would be groovy."

CHAPTER SIX

Chiun did not wish to leave the hotel at night. The northern cold of the Finger Lakes district of New York was too much for a Korean. Thus he stated.

"Sinanju goes to twenty below zero during the winter. You told me that yourself," Remo complained. "And this is spring."

"Ah, but in Sinanju, it is a clean cold."

"I don't understand," said Remo, understanding all too well. The payments for not visiting the birthplace of Barbra Streisand were coming due.

"Your ignorance is not my burden," said Chiun and would say no more. A typical response, thought Remo.

At dawn, Remo asked Chiun if he had anything against dirty mornings. Or did the Master of Sinanju need a clean morning to go with his clean cold before he would leave the hotel?

Chiun refused to descend to pretty bickering and tendentiousness. It was enough that he was going to examine the spot along the canal.

The morning sun over dew-fresh grass was refreshing, so they walked.

"Little Father," said Remo as they crossed an iron bridge over the canal, "I am confused."

"The beginning of knowledge."

"Everything I know about our skills tells me it takes time."

"Much time," said Chiun.

"Is it possible to achieve minimum skills in a day?"

Chiun shook his head. A gentle breeze caught his wispy beard.

"No," he said. "It is not possible."

The bridge blended into a sidewalk, and they moved underneath a row of green budding trees with small houses set on oversized lots on both sides of the street. The fragments of front lawns were muddy. It had rained during the night.

"Then how could inexperienced people smuggle a field weapon through a detection device, and learn the use of firearms in a day?" asked Remo. "How could they do such a thing?"

Chiun smiled. "There seems to be a contradiction there, does there not?" he said.

"There does," Remo said.

"There is none," said Chiun, and he explained.

"Once, a long time ago, the House of Sinanju was summoned by an emperor of China, a cunning man, a wealthy man, a man of great perception but no wisdom, of great military victories but no courage. He was, in brief, not Korean in his virtues.

"The emperor requested the services of the House of Sinanju. This was not the emperor who failed to pay for services, but the great, great grandfather of that emperor who one day would commission a Master of Sinanju and not pay, thus depriving the babies of the village of Sinanju of food."

"Yes, yes, get on with it. I know the story about the emperor who didn't pay for the hit," said Remo.

"It is an important part of any story dealing with China," Chiun said.

"Little Father, I know that the village of Sinanju is very poor, and that it has no crops, and in order to get

71

food for the children and the aged, you hired your-
selves out as assassins, and anyone who doesn't pay is
really murdering your babies."

"It is a little thing to you. They are not your children."

"That was over six hundred years ago."

"A crime, unlike pain, does not diminish with time."

"Right," Remo said. "It was a horrible, undiminished
crime, and no emperor of China should ever be
trusted."

"Correct. But this was his great, great grandfather,"
Chiun continued. "The emperor had a problem. He
wished to wage a very special assault against a king
beyond his borders. The palace of the king was on a
high mountain. It could not be assaulted by soldiers
without great loss. The emperor did not wish to lose
many of his fine troops. But he had peasants, more than
enough peasants, who in that year of crop failure would
starve to death anyway. Could the world's most illus-
trious and magnificent assassins, the perfection of mankind, the ultimate in what mere mortals might possibly
achieve, in brief, could the Master of Sinanju train
peasants to assault this castle so that prime troops
would not have to be lost?"

"The Chinese emperor called your ancestors the perfection of mankind?" asked Remo incredulously.

"That is the way the story was told to me," said
Chiun.

"But you said Chinese emperor is another word for
liar."

"Even a liar must tell the truth sometimes.

"The emperor said the special assault must be con-
ducted within the month as the king had planned to

move a great treasure out of the palace on the mountain. The ancestor of Chiun thought hard and long. What makes a warrior and what makes a peasant? Is it the eyes? No. All men have eyes. Is it the muscles? No. All men have muscles that can be trained briefly. Then why should it take years to train a good soldier? The Master of Sinanju thought and thought.

"Why was the House of Sinanju superior to all other assassins? What made Sinanju perfection among flaws? What made the House of Sinanuju respected and revered throughout the world?"

"The House of Sinanju is known by maybe ten people today, Little Father," Remo said.

"This is the way the story was told to me," said Chiun.

"Then one day, the Master saw a soldier push a peasant off a road. The soldier was slight of build. The peasant was large and strong. Yet the peasant did not strike back. And then the Master knew what he could do, in a very short time. What was different between the peasant and the soldier was the mind. That was the difference. Only the mind. The peasant surely could have slain the soldier but he could not see himself doing it. His mind did not have it.

"So the Master had artists draw pictures of the palace and the mountain. And he gathered the peasants before him and he spoke to them as they looked at the pictures. And as they looked, he had artists draw in their likenesses scaling the mountain, one on another. And he had artists draw in their likenesses killing the king's soldiers. And he talked to them until he had them seeing in their mind that they could do this thing. And at the end they believed that not only could they

73

do this thing, but already had done this thing. And he had them chant together the signals they would hear.

"And so they marched from the emperor's lands to the land of the king who lived in the palace on the mountain. And every day on the march, they chanted the orders to themselves and saw themselves scale the mountain.

"And when the day arrived, they approached the mountain with the assurance of soldiers and scaled the mountain and overcame the fortifications, losing some men, but not as many as might be expected. This was due to the planning of the Master of Sinanju.

"But lo, inside the palace, they fell to their knees because after all, they were peasants and had never seen the inside of a palace. And they wandered around, frightened and confused, and were slaughtered by the mere household guard, for they had not seen themselves inside the palace. They only visualized themselves assaulting it.

"So," finished Chiun, "were they skilled or were they not?"

"They were and they weren't."

"Exactly."

"Then these people are skilled and not skilled."

"Exactly."

"How can I tell that to Smith?" Remo asked. "He is already greatly disturbed."

"That will pass."

"How do you know, Little Father?"

"I know. Did you not see his eyes or his fingers or the way he looks at the sky?"

"Smitty never looked at the sky in his life. He never

did anything but play with his computers. He's a man without a soul."

Chiun smiled. "Perhaps, but he is a man."

"No," said Remo. "You're not telling me it's his time of life."

"Indeed it is," Chiun said. "He suffers now because life is telling him it is the beginning of being over. It is almost over and he was never there. But this shall pass, because it is only a moment, and he shall return to the illusion that most men have: that they will never die. And under that illusion, he will return to normal."

"A bitter heartless machine," said Remo.

"Exactly," said Chiun. "There are worse emperors to work for."

The sidewalk ended a few yards past the last frame house. Remo and Chiun walked along the side of the road, and if one watched them from behind, he would see that the American now walked with the gliding motion of the Oriental, their arms and shoulders moving as if they were twins.

They turned off the road at a small dirt path that led through a stand of birch, and down a small hill. Both men moved effortlessly.

"Tell me," asked Remo. "Whatever became of the assault on the palace?"

"It had a good ending. The Master led a small party to the treasure room and guided them into retrieving it. They made their way down the mountain and returned to the emperor with the treasure.

"And the peasants?"

"They were killed."

"How can you say it was a good ending?"

"The emperor paid."

"If it was just money, why didn't the Master just keep the king's treasure?"

"Because we are not thieves," yelled Chiun.

"You stole from the king!"

With that, Chiun gushed forth a stream of Korean, a few words of which Remo recognized. Stupid. White man. Ingrate. Invincibly ignorant. Bird droppings. And one more, which Remo recognized from constant use. It was a saying of the House of Sinanju: "You can take mud from the river, but you cannot make of it a diamond. Be satisfied with a brick."

A large clearing loomed ahead and Remo pressed forward until he suddenly realized he was walking alone. He turned around and Chiun stood twenty feet behind him, near a large rock. There was a small clearing around the rock as if a deer had settled there for the night and nothing grew again.

Remo motioned with his head for Chiun to keep up with him, but Chiun did not move.

"C'mon," Remo said. "The training site must be just up ahead. The girl said it was at the bottom of the hill."

Chiun raised a finger. "That clearing up ahead was not the place," he said. "This was the place."

Remo trotted back to the rock and looked around. There was the rock, about twice the height of a man, the small muddy clearing that looked more like a widening of the path, and nothing else.

"How do you know?" said Remo.

Chiun pointed to a small flattened section of the rock at about his shoulder height. The section was smooth, about the size of a matchbook cover, and looked as if someone had chipped it away with another rock.

"It is time," said Chiun, "to leave the service of this emperor. Come, I can find employment for you, too. We must leave. There is always work for assassins. Do not worry about your income."

He touched his long fingernail to the flattened section of rock.

"This tells anyone fortunate enough to know," he said, "that the time has come to seek another benefactor, to serve elsewhere. Leave America to its own devices."

Remo felt his stomach knot, a breath surge up into his throat.

"What the hell are you talking about? I'd never quit when I'm needed." But the Master of Sinanju had already turned, and was looking up toward the sky.

CHAPTER SEVEN

Henry Pfeiffer was rearranging the price marker on the leg of lamb in his butcher shop window on Ballard Street in Seneca Falls when a coed from Patton College entered and smilingly told him he was going to kill two people.

"I beg your pardon," he said in an accent tinged with the gutturals of Bremerhaven, Germany, where he was born. "Who are you? What are you talking about?"

"My name is Joan Hacker. I'm a senior at Patton College. And you're going to try to kill two men for the revolution. Only you may not be able to, but you're the best we can get right now."

"Uh, sit down, sit down. Can I get you a glass of water?" Henry Pfeiffer wiped his beefy hands on his stained apron and guided the young girl to a chair.

"It's really very simple," said Joan Hacker. "You can't make an omelet without breaking eggs. We've got to break eggs. I'm giving up a meaningful relationship, and I mean, meaningful. I may never get that much of a relationship again. But I'm doing it for the revolution."

"Perhaps some Alka Seltzer? Or schnapps? And then we phone the hospital, *ja?*"

"Nein," said Joan Hacker who knew a little bit of German. "We don't have time. They're a bit up the canal now, and you will have good cover before they reach the road. I got them there. I mean, I did most of the work. I would have told you earlier, but we didn't want to give you much time to think about it. We wanted to wait for them to get there. We're giving you cover. You ought to be grateful."

"Little girl, you will go to the hospital if I phone?"

"No, Captain Gruenwald. S.S. Captain Oskar Gruenwald. I will not go to the hospital. I will wait for you."

Blood drained away from the heavy face of the butcher on Ballard Street. He steadied himself on the clean glass case.

"Little girl, do you know what you're talking about?"

"Yes, I do, Captain. You looked marvelous in your S.S. uniform. That's all right. I don't mind that you were a Nazi. We're not against Nazis anymore, what with Israel and everything. Naziism was just another form of colonialism. America is worse."

Oskar Gruenwald who had not been called Oskar Gruenwald since one wintery day in 1945 when he took the uniform from a dead Wehrmacht sergeant and surrendered to a British patrol outside Antwerp, locked the door of his shop so no one else could enter. Then he spoke to the young girl.

"Miss. Let me explain."

"We don't have time for explanations," said Joan Hacker. "And don't try anything funny. If anything happens to me, your wife and family will get it."

"Miss," said Gruenwald, lowering his massive frame into a chair beside the girl. "You do not look like a cruel person. You have never killed anyone, have you?"

"The revolution hasn't required me to do that yet, but don't think I'd cop out."

"Miss, I have seen bodies stacked like mountains. Mothers with children, frozen together in ditches. I have walked on ground that oozed blood because of so many buried alive underneath. It is a horrible insane thing, this killing, and to think that you take it so lightly as a form of social medicine is beyond the anguished ken of all mankind. Please listen to me. You have discovered my secret. So be it. But do not put blood on your hands. It is a terrible thing, this killing."

"You're irrelevant," said Joan Hacker. "We not only have your secret identity which the West German government would be very interested in, but we know that your son and grandchildren are right now in Buenos Aires, and they would look very unattractive after a bomb went off in their living room. On the other hand, if you do this thing for the revolution, no one will be the wiser."

"How can I get through to you? I will not kill again," said Gruenwald, knowing, even as he said it, that once again he had been cozened into murder. The first time, he did not know what he was doing. He was seventeen and his country had a leader who promised a new prosperity and pride. There were bands and marching and songs and Oskar went to war with the Waffen SS. Indeed, he did look good in his uniform. He was thin and blond and even of teeth. Before his twentieth birthday, he was an old man and a murderer. Oskar ordered people to dig ditches and then filled the ditches with the diggers. Oskar burned churches with the parishioners still inside. And the strange thing happened to him that happens to almost every person who, face to face, commits mass murder. He stopped caring about his own life and started taking incredible chances. He rose to captain and then was assigned to a special assassination squad, this old young man. Years later, he realized that people who kill wantonly seek their own death as well, and this is mistakenly called courage. Years later, when he had managed to build a new life and could see the massive horror at a distance, he knew he would never harm another person again. It was very hard learning to forgive yourself, but if you worked with children and donated much time to those who needed your time, bit by bit you could become human again and learn to build and love and care. And those were precious things.

Throughout the years, there was one reassurance. The insanity of the Second World War would never be repeated, the mass murder for the sake of extermination would never be again. And then, to his horror, Oskar Gruenwald saw the insanity beginning again, like a dormant disease that suddenly sprouts a new boil.

People, many of them well-educated, forgot World War II. Playing little mind games with themselves, they decided that a massive military bombing which killed a thousand people in ten days was worse than a war which killed more than fifty million people. And if it suited their purpose to support a charge of racism, then everyone forgot the hundred thousand Germans killed in one raid on Dresden, and said America would not have bombed a European country as it bombed Vietnam.

It was as if the world's greatest holocaust was forgotten because it was a quarter of a century old, and now the new Nazis were on the march and they called their master race "the liberated" and their new world war was "the revolution." Their stupidity was enough to make grown men cry.

"Little girl," said Oskar Gruenwald to the pert coed

who had threatened the lives of his offspring. "You think you are doing good. You think you will make things better by killing. But I tell you from experience, the only thing you will do is kill. I too thought I was improving the world and all I did was kill."

"But you didn't have consciousness raising," said Joan Hackett, sure of her enlightenment.

"We did, but they were called rallies," said Oskar Gruenwald, now Henry Pfeiffer. "The minute you kill other than to save your own life, the minute you kill for some new social order, then you have nothing but insanity."

"I can't reason with you," said Joan Hacker, very annoyed and fervently wishing some of her friends were here to help her argue. "Are you going to do what we want or are you going to be exposed and watch your offspring get offed?"

"Offed is killed, is it not?" asked the aging Gruenwald.

"Yes. Like in 'off the pigs,' " said Joan Hacker.

Oskar Gruenwald lowered his head. His past was coming home again.

"All right, Gauleiter," he said, referring to an old Nazi rank for political officers. "I will do as you say."

"What's a Gauleiter?" asked Joan Hacker, and Oskar Gruenwald cried and laughed at the same time.

CHAPTER EIGHT

Remo was stunned. He was furious. He looked at the small piece of shaved rock and then back at Chiun. What angered him was Chiun's self-assured conviction that Remo should understand immediately why they must flee and Chiun's refusal to explain further.

Chiun turned slowly, as if reading Remo's thoughts, and said, "I am a teacher, not a nursemaid. You have eyes but you see not. You have a mind but you think not. You see the evidence and you stand there like a blubbering child, demanding to know why we must flee. And yet I tell you, you know."

"And I tell you I don't know."

"Hit the rock," said Chiun. "Take a piece off."

Remo cracked down flathanded and sheared a chunk to the ground. Chiun nodded to the shaved section, its lines similar to the section which had so astounded him in the first place.

"All right," said Chiun, as though granting Remo his most childish indulgence. "Now you know."

"Now I don't know," said Remo.

Chiun turned and walked down the path, muttering in Korean. Remo caught a few words, basically dealing with the inability of anyone to transform mud into diamonds. Remo followed Chiun.

"I'm not leaving. That's it, little father."

"Yes, I know. You love America. America has been so good to you. It taught you the secrets of Sinanju; it devoted its best years raising you to a level that no white man has every achieved before. A mere handful of all men in history were as skillful as you are and you love America, not the teacher who made you so. So be it. I am not hurt. I am enlightened."

"It is not a question of loving either you or my country, little father. You both have my loyalty."

"That is something one tells his concubine and wife, not the Master of Sinanju."

Remo started to explain when Chiun's bony hand raised.

"Are you beginning to forget everything?" asked Chiun and then Remo noticed it, down the path, that very special stillness he could normally sense in his blood.

The stillness was behind a bush, perhaps fifty yards away. Chiun made a birdlike motion indicating he would stand where he was while Remo was to circle round whatever was creating the stillness in the wet spring fields of the Finger Lakes region.

Remo knew Chiun would pretend to walk forward and not move; pretend to cut into the bush and not move; seem to do what he was not doing and thus totally absorb the interest of whoever was behind the bush.

Remo moved easily off the path, as quietly as a morning sigh, across the rocks, body weighting only against that which did not snap or creak or rustle. He did not feel at home in the forest because like the true assassin, his home was the city where the targets invariably lived. Yet he could use this shrub—undergrowth and trees and soggy loamy soil—because the forest, too, was his tool.

Remo saw the flash of a white shirt behind leafy

green and kept moving at an angle. He saw the top of a reddish bald head and then a beefy neck. A rifle stock pressed into an overlapping red cheek and the barrel went forward, aimed at a kimono fifty yards away. Remo moved up to the man. The man's knee sunk into the wet spring soil. He was in kneeling position. An adequate-enough way to fire a rifle and an even better way to lose a finger.

Oskar Gruenwald was not thinking about his fingers as he tried to sight on the kimono. He was wondering why he was having such a difficult time. He could not have forgotten what he was taught, not even after a quarter of a century. He could not have forgotten what was drilled into him and drilled into him and drilled into him. If you have two men, you pick the one behind the first, bang, squeeze off the next two shots against the leader, and then the fourth shot to finish the man you hit first. That was how he had been trained. His targets were the favorites of the Waffen S.S. Lithuanians or Ukrainians. It didn't matter. Oskar's instructor took him to the outskirts of a small village and told him to pick off men going to market. That was the first day of instruction. Oskar mistakenly shot the first, and the second had time to get away. It was then his instructor said:

"You see. What you did wrong was not only give someone time to get away, but you committed the cardinal sin of a sniper ambush. You stopped to think. You must never stop to think, but must have your shots planned in advance. That way all you have to do is aim."

It had worked well. It worked in Russia, then the

Ukraine, then Poland, and then back to the borders of Germany. It worked his last day in Waffen S.S. uniform before he changed to the uniform of the regular Army and took a new name, which had lasted until that morning in his shop.

But now it was not working. There were his two targets, the Oriental in back and the American in front. All right, pop one off at the Oriental. But he was beginning to move off the path. He was retreating. No. He was advancing. What the hell was that little yellow man doing? Now there was no more American. Where was the American? He wasn't on the path. To hell with it. Get the Oriental and then hunt the American. The old, cold feeling of competence returned to Oskar Gruenwald. The mechanical competence of the professional killer.

He was just squeezing off a shot at the center of the kimono, when he realized this would be impossible to do. One needed a trigger finger for that sort of thing and Oskar Gruenwald now had only a bloody stump. No pain. Just no finger.

"Hi there, fella," Remo said. "I'd shake but you can't. This yours?" he said and offered the shocked sniper his finger back.

"Aaaargh," said former S.S. Captain Oskar Gruenwald, suddenly feeling the delayed pain where his finger used to join his hand.

"All right, if you don't want me to dismember you piece by piece, tell me who sent you," said Remo.

The sniper looked at his right index finger—in his left palm.

"C'mon," Remo said. "I don't have all day."

"A girl. She was a foolish girl. Do not blame her."

"Her name?"

"There has been enough death and you will kill her, I know."

"Her name?" said Remo, and it was not really a question.

Gruenwald lunged for the rifle with his left hand, but then his left hand no longer worked. He did not even see the American move, the stroke was so swift.

"The girl?"

"Her name was Joan Hacker," said Oskar Gruenwald. "But please don't kill her."

"I don't kill if I don't have to," said Remo.

"When one kills that becomes all he does".

"It's only you amateurs who are menaces," said Remo.

Oskar Gruenwald snarled back. "I was not an amateur, sir. Waffen S.S. Captain."

"And I'm sure you were a very good Waffen whatever-it-is," said Remo consolingly, putting him away with a head shot.

Chiun glided past Remo with a casual glance at the fat corpse sinking into the damp soil. The head stroke must have been perfect, thought Remo, or there would have been comment.

"First fat. Then thin," said Chiun. "Then the dead animals and then all my work for nothing, because of your impatience."

"Now I understand," said Remo sarcastically. "First fat, then thin, then the dead animals, and then all your work for nothing. Why didn't you say so instead of talking in riddles?"

"Even the morning sun is a riddle to a fool," said Chiun. "Now comes thin."

"Of course, thin," said Remo. "What else comes after fat? I mean I could have told you that even before my training. Now thin."

CHAPTER NINE

"You don't think I'm too thin?" said Rodney Pintwhistle.

Joan Hacker did not think Rodney was too thin at all. She thought he was esthetic. Joan didn't go for all those muscles bulging around. She went for a man who was lean and lithe.

"Really?" said Rodney Pintwhistle, a blush coming up behind a face of acne. He patted his almost empty sweater. "I mean, you really don't think I'm too thin?"

"I'll show you how thin I think you are," said Joan Hacker. "Come on up to my room and I'll show you."

Rodney Pintwhistle, whose main sexual activity was stroking himself while imagining coeds like Joan Hacker inviting him up to her room, coughed up his strawberry milkshake onto the formica table top. People in the student union looked around. A waiter patted Rodney on the back.

"C'mon, Rodney, let's get out of here," said Joan, flaunting her full and bouncing breasts as she rose.

"Maybe I'd better have another milkshake."

"Maybe you'd better come with me," said Joan, grabbing him by the wrist. She jerked. Rodney came.

On the path to the dormitory, Rodney suggested that they get to know each other better.

"This is the best way," said Joan, tugging his wrist.

Maybe they should stop and talk more?

"Talking is better after," said Joan.

Rodney suddenly remembered he had a class.

"Cut it," said Joan.

Rodney couldn't. You see he already had two cuts and if he got a third cut, he might get below a B and then he wouldn't make the dean's list.

"You never made dean's list, Rodney," she said.

But this year Rodney had a chance. Really he did. He was taking easier courses and this year he really had a chance and if there was one thing he really wanted to do more than anything else in college, it was to make dean's list one year, at least one year. That's what he really wanted to do.

"You're full of crap, Rodney," said Joan Hacker, for if there was anything that raised her anger, it was weakness in someone else. It brought out the tiger in her, that tiger which seemed to disappear when someone else assumed command.

She tugged Rodney into the dormitory and then pushed him up the two flights of steps to her floor and then into her room. Her roommate sat on the bed, legs tucked under her bare bottom, a sweat shirt covering the raised knee tops.

"Out," said Joan Hacker, in a rare display of authority.

The roommate blinked, and never having seen the tiger in Joan before, dutifully got up, apologized for being there, and left the room. Joan locked the door. Rodney giggled.

"The nearer the bone, the sweeter the meat," said Joan, repeating a phrase she had heard in high school and resented years later as being oppressive and exploitative.

Rodney backed against the window. Joan advanced. Rodney covered his groin. Joan yanked his hand away and stroked. Rodney brushed her hand away. Joan kissed him on his scrawny neck. Rodney said that tickled.

Joan grabbed his neck and brought his head down forcefully to hers. She invaded his mouth. She manipulated one hand behind his neck and the other in front of his trousers. She manipulated, she worked, and when she had him ready, she eased him to the bed. Ploing. It was all over. She fell on him.

"You're magnificent, Rodney," gasped Joan.

Rodney averred that he hardly did anything at all. He was just a natural, he guessed.

"You must have hundreds of women, Rodney."

No, not really. Could Joan believe that she was the first woman he had had at Patton College?

"No. I couldn't believe that. You're so magnificent. But you don't love me."

Rodney felt no passionate warmth toward this attractive coed who had transformed his fantasies into reality, but having been accused of not loving her, his reaction was instinctive and immediate.

"That's not true. I love you."

"No, you don't."

"Yes, I do. I really do. I think you're . . . you're swell," said Rodney, and this was not like his fantasies at all.

"If you loved me, you'd protect me."

"I'll protect you," said Rodney.

"Now, you won't. You're just using me for my body. You're exploiting me."

"I'm not exploiting you. I'll protect you."

"Really, Rodney? Do you promise? You're not just stringing me along, are you?"

Rodney was not stringing her along and his promise was his bond. Thus it was that Rodney Pintwhistle, who was excused from gym class because of asthma, chronic bronchitis, anemia and what one gym instructor called "an awesome lack of coordination," found himself that afternoon standing before a hotel room with a knife in his hands, threatening America's primary secret enforcer and the greatest assassin ever to walk the face of the earth, the Master of Sinanju.

Rodney took on the Oriental first because he looked easier.

"What are you looking at?" yelled Rodney, waving the knife at the Oriental in the flowing kimono.

"My hotel room," said the Oriental. "Please be so kind as to let me pass."

"You're not passing anywhere, Charlie."

"Have I offended you?" asked Chiun.

"Yeah. You've been bothering Joan Hacker. If you guys don't stop this, I'll . . . I'll maybe use this thing."

"We promise to stop," said the Master of Sinanju.

"Oh," said Rodney Pintwhistle. "I mean, really."

"Really," said Chiun.

"What about your buddy?"

"He promises too," said Chiun.

"Well, then I guess it's all settled," said Rodney. "You two guys aren't bad at all."

"Where is Miss Hacker?" asked Remo.

"None of your business," said Rodney, and then feeling sorry for the taller man, said: "I mean, she's on campus. But you won't bother her, will you?"

"Do I look like someone who'd go where he's not wanted?"

Rodney had to admit, the man didn't. Rodney fairly

glided back to campus. The new Rodney Pintwhistle—lover, strong man, a man before whom women melted and men grovelled. Joan was surprised to see him.

"Oh, Rodney, what are you doing here?" she asked as he strolled into her room.

"Came to tell you you'll have no trouble from those two anymore."

"The Oriental and the good-looking guy?"

"He wasn't so good-looking."

"You're sure you got the right two?"

"I'm sure," Rodney said. "They apologized." He stuffed his hands in his pockets and waited for gratitude. Joan Hacker rose from the bed with a roundhouse swing at the side of his head. It connected with a crack. Rodney hurtled back into and over a chair. He held the side of his head.

"All right for you," Rodney cried. "I'm telling. I'm telling. I'm telling that you gave me a knife and asked me to threaten someone."

"You lied to me, punk," yelled Joan, kicking at the scrawny leg protecting his acne covered face.

"I didn't. I didn't. They apologized."

"You never even saw them. Liar. Liar."

"Don't hit," yelled Rodney. "I have fragile bones."

"Hit? I'll punch your heart out, you son of a bitch. I'll punch your frigging heart out. You tell anyone, I'll punch your heart out."

And Rodney promised. The lad who had backed down the Destroyer and the Master of Sinanju promised he would not tell a soul, but in return he, too, wanted a pledge.

"Just don't hit."

CHAPTER TEN

Joan Hacker was afraid. She dawdled down the street to the football stadium like a toddler forced to go to bed.

First of all, it was not her fault. Rodney was the only thin, really thin, boy she knew. She couldn't be expected to know right off that he would come back with a nonsense story. How could she know that? She did everything she could.

And besides. Hadn't the German done what he was supposed to do? Everyone was talking about how old Henry Pfeiffer had been attacked by some strange beast that had bitten off his finger and crushed his head. Everyone. Absolutely everyone, and she hadn't said a word to anyone. She had done exactly as she was told. It wasn't as if she hadn't tried.

Joan Hacker stopped in front of the rising concrete structure, so noisy on football Saturdays in autumn, and so quiet now. So . . . so imposing looking, she thought.

She had done everything she was asked and now, because of that stinking Rodney Pintwhistle, she wouldn't be allowed to take any more real part in the revolution. It was downright oppressive. And she had done everything right.

Joan reached into her windbreaker pocket, carefully opened the metal container and pinched some of the powder between her right fingertips. She withdrew her hand, put the powder in her left palm, and raised the palm to her left nostril. She sniffed hard. A stinging sensation showed that she had inhaled one of the cocaine crystals instead of just the powder. Her eyes watered. After a few moments, the pain passed, and in its place came a new resolve and new courage. Joan Hacker marched through the deserted darkened arch of Patton Memorial Field. She would not be oppressed, even though she was dealing with the Third World. But the man wasn't all that Third World, not into it really. He had said something nasty when she asked if he were Vietnamese. Very nasty.

Joan entered the sunlight of the football field, her steps crunching on the cinder track. She looked along the Patton side of the stands. He wasn't there. Glancing toward the visitors' side, she saw him, standing right dab on the fifty-yard line. Now that wasn't a very good place for a revolutionary meeting. The forest by the canal was better. A car in an alley was better. Almost any place would be better. After all, if he could make a mistake like this, then who was he to blame her for Rodney?

"Hi. Uhh, I've got a bit of . . . well, not so nice news," said Joan as she reached the man in midfield. He was slightly shorter than she, with smooth yellow skin and hazel eyes. He wore a black business suit with a white shirt and black tie, like one of those little Japanese computer salesmen, only she had better not call him a Japanese again, because he had gotten angry about that too. Not *angry* angry, but a cold quiet angry. The man nodded to her.

"I, well, I tried. And it wasn't my fault."

The Oriental face was stone.

"Really, it wasn't. I, well, I got the skinny one as

95

you said, and the fat one worked well. Let me tell you. He did make an attempt on the two reactionaries, and they were there at the spot you told me to tell them about. You know, where the soul brothers trained and everything."

"They were coming from the path or going into it?" asked the Oriental, in a thin, cold voice.

"Coming, because Gruenwald or Pfeiffer or whatever he was, left after they left."

"Good. They saw the rock."

Joan Hacker smiled.

"I did well on that, then?"

"Truly revolutionary," said the Oriental and he smiled. It did not look like an approving smile to Joan, rather a contemptuous smile. But who could really tell with the Third World?

"Well, after that I recruited the skinniest, absolutely the skinniest student on campus. He promised me he would threaten those two. He did. I swear it."

The Oriental nodded.

"But then he came back without even a scratch on him and he lied to me. He told me they apologized."

"You did very well," said the Oriental.

"I did?" said Joan in amazement. "I thought he never even went near them. I mean, I could punch out Rodney myself. Why would they apologize?"

"Why wouldn't they, my child? I mean, my revolutionary heroine. The typhoon uproots trees and shatters boulders, but it does not harm the grass."

"That's Mao?"

"It is not the Chinaman. You have done well. There is more to do, and you must join me in doing it, because you are a great revolutionary heroine. You will

96

come with me. But one thing. If the young American or the old man should seek you again, you must tell them the dead animals are next."

"The dead animals are next," repeated Joan Hacker with a little nod. "I don't understand it."

"It's revolutionary," the Oriental said. "A good revolutionary never asks questions, but strives to help the revolution."

"But why don't we just off them?" asked Joan.

"Because it is written that all must be quiet while the typhoon roars."

She looked puzzled. "I know I'm not supposed to ask questions, but what does that mean? About the typhoon?"

"You have done well, so I will tell you. The typhoon that has now come is dangerous in any alley or room or building. That is why we stand here this sunny day in the middle of a football field. When one speaks to our typhoon, one does not send a telegram or write a letter or make a telephone call. He sends the message in the way it will be understood. A sign that another typhoon has passed. Perhaps a chip on a rock that could only be made by the same training. A fat man and a thin man to show that the extremes of weight are no problem. They are an offering, their lives are."

"And the dead animals?" Joan asked.

"That is a secret," said the Oriental with that same superior smile. "It is a revolutionary secret."

"And I'm sharing it. With a real revolutionary. Not just some talkers. I mean, I'm really in it."

"You are really in it," said the quiet Oriental. There was that smile again.

CHAPTER ELEVEN

Dr. Harold Smith sat before the console of the computer outlet in Folcroft Sanitarium, a vast estate on the Long Island Sound, whose employees thought it to be a research center—all the employees but one. That employee—Dr. Smith—could, by pressing his computer keys, pull from its memory banks information on all types of crime, domestic and international, that could threaten the United States. With a telephone call, he could place into the field hundreds of agents to gather information for CURE, an organization they did not know existed.

Now, as Smith sat before his console, he did not know what button to press or whom to call. He was bothered. Was he all right? Yesterday, he had thrown an ashtray at a secretary. And every call from Remo asked if he were all right. Today Remo had questioned him about the advisability of sending in other personnel to Patton.

"Why the hell couldn't you wait, Smitty? What's wrong with you?"

Well, he couldn't wait. The world was ready to take another major step toward peace with the signing of the antiterrorist pact, and any more terrorist action could shatter that peace. Dr. Smith had an obligation to everything he ever learned, everything he ever loved, to make sure that peace happened.

"I'll decide that, Remo," he had said. "I am feeling perfectly fine."

And then Remo had told him the riddle. It came from Chiun, who often spoke in riddles, but did this riddle really have a meaning? A typhoon is silent when another typhoon passes? What did that mean?

A buzzer sounded in Smith's desk. Smith removed the special phone from the top drawer and slumped back into his soft rocking seat.

"Yes sir," he said.

"Are congratulations in order?" the familiar voice asked.

"For what, Mister President?"

"Didn't your special man get to the headquarters of those terrorists?"

"Yes sir, he did. But we may not have eliminated the cause. We may just be in a dormant period with the terrorists."

"What do you mean?"

"I am told there will be no terrorist activity because . . . because one typhoon is silent when another passes."

There was a pause on the end of the line, then: "I don't understand that."

"Neither do I, sir. But it comes from one of our men familiar with this sort of thing."

"Hmmm. Well, at any rate, we have a hiatus?"

"Yes sir. I believe so."

"Good. I'll pass that on to our negotiator. Only four more days till the antiterrorist conference at the U.N. With luck, it'll be an in-and-out kind of thing. Sort of *wham, bam, thank you, ma'am,* and the world's air-ways are safe again."

"Yes sir," said Smith, annoyed at the allusion to sex. He had thought this President was above that sort of thing. Still, the President had great pressures on him in his quest for peace. Dr. Harold Smith must take a personal hand to make sure that nothing happened to foil that quest.

On a United States destroyer off the Atlantic coast, Colonel Anderson was greeted with congratulations by Colonel Huang and Colonel Petrovich.

Anderson dropped his briefcase on the green felt table in the ward room, and in a lackluster manner took the offered hands. "We'll finish the agreements today," he said, "then check the language with our governments and meet the day after tomorrow to finish up."

"There will be no problem," said Petrovich, "now that this new terrorist mess has been cleared up."

"Yes," said Huang.

Anderson sighed and looked at both men, eye to eye, then asked: "What makes you think we've cleared it up?"

Petrovich smiled. "Don't be coy with us. You people stopped them dead. The hijacking last weekend must have been the first time you used your new system. We know it was the new wave of terrorists because they got that machine gun past your detection devices. We do have sources in your country, you know."

Huang nodded. "Now tell us how you did it?" he asked.

"Would you believe me if I said I do not know how?" Anderson said.

"No," said Petrovich. "Not a word of it."

"I might suspect you were telling the truth," said Huang, "but I wouldn't believe a word of it."

Anderson shrugged. "Well, since you two aren't going to believe me, let me tell you what you definitely won't believe. I have been instructed by my superiors to tell you this so you will be aware of what we are facing. I get it from the highest authority that this terrorist force is dormant. Only dormant, because something similar to it is functioning. Now hold on. Don't laugh so hard. This is what I was told. I was told that one typhoon is quiet when another typhoon passes."

Petrovich guffawed and slapped the table. He looked to Huang for support, but there was none. Colonel Huang was not smiling.

"The image you used was quiet typhoons?" he questioned softly.

Anderson nodded and even he smiled. But Huang did not smile, not even when the last few technical points on the accords were reached, not even when all three shook hands and congratulated themselves on a job well done, and separated amidst promises to meet two days hence with approvals on the language for the antiterrorist pact.

Huang remained glum, even onto the plane to Canada, where he was to meet with his government's top political officer. On the flight he did some calculating, namely whether to risk his career by relaying a fairy tale, an old tool of the Chinese emperors to create fear in their armies. Colonel Huang was not so far beyond reproach that he could relay what he suspected with impunity.

Huang gazed into the cloudless blue sky.

One typhoon is silent when another typhoon passes, he thought. Yes, he remembered. He remembered very well. There was a village in Korea from which the greatest assassins in the world came. These assassins were employed by the emperors to keep the army in line. It was an old Chinese custom to have others do your fighting for you. The Revolution ended that. The Chinese did their own fighting now.

But in the olden times, emperors played enemies off against each other, and hired their real fighting men. And the men they hired knew that there was another force that would destroy them, should they fail to serve faithfully.

What was that village's name? It was in the friendly part of Korea. On the water facing China. Sinanju. That was it. Sinanju. The assassins of Sinanju—and the greatest were the Masters of Sinanju, one master each lifetime.

He had once visited the museum and gallery in the heart of what was once the Forbidden City. And there in a glass case was a seven-foot sword, and the legend read that it had been wielded by the Master of Sinanju. Not long ago, Peking had buzzed with the rumors that the Premier's life had been saved by just such a Master, using that very sword.

He had first heard of Sinanju from his grandfather, when Huang was a very small boy. He had asked what would happen if one assassin from Sinanju should take up arms in opposition to another assassin from Sinanju. His grandfather had told him that one typhoon is silent when another passes.

Young Huang thought about that, then asked what would happen if the other typhoon was not silent.

"Then stay away from the dead animals for no mortal can survive that holocaust," his grandfather had said. And when Huang had complained that he did not understand the answer, his grandfather would only say: "Thus was it written."

Of course, his grandfather was an oppressor of the peasants and an enemy of the people and naturally he would have a vested interest in peddling reactionary myths.

But today, the masses had exploded all the reactionary myths. This was a new China and Colonel Huang was part of it. He would stay part of it. He would not repeat the silly reactionary fairy tale to the political officer he would meet in Canada.

But as he looked into the blue sky, Colonel Huang wondered just how much mystery remained beyond the ken of Chairman Mao's little red book.

CHAPTER TWELVE

"Just look at this place, will you? Just look at this place."

The buxom redhead, wearing only a gray Mickey Mouse sweatshirt, was near tears, so Remo looked at the place. It was a mess. The small dormitory room was strewn with torn papers. Pages ripped from books littered the desk and the bed. Broken covers of books were everywhere.

"What happened?" Remo asked.

"That Joan did it," the girl said bitterly. "She comes back up here, as high and mighty as you please, and announces, mind you, announces, that she is joining the fucking revolutionary army, and leaving this fucking school, and I can go fuck myself, and then I went out of the room for a minute and when I came back, it looked like this and she was fucking marching out."

"Where'd she go?" Remo asked.

"She told me she was ripping off the pig college's books so that they couldn't poison anyone else's mind with their Fascist lies," the redhead said, ignoring Remo. She stood in the middle of the floor, stamping her feet like an angry child, and as her bare feet hit the uncarpeted floor, her breasts jiggled.

"But where'd she go?"

"And it wouldn't be so bad if they were just her books, but they were mine too. And now I'm going to have to pay for them. The bitch."

"Oh, the bitch," Remo agreed.

"The dirty bitch."

"Oh, the dirty bitch," Remo agreed.

"She said she was going to New York City."

"Oh, the dirty bitch is going to New York City," Remo said. "But where in New York City?"

"I don't know and I don't care. Look what she did to my room. I hope that toothache of hers abscesses her whole fucking head."

"I'll help you straighten up," Remo said.

"Would you? Say, that's really nice of you. You wouldn't want to ball, would you? I've got body paints we can play with."

"No, thank you. I'm saving it until I get married," Remo said, as he began to scoop up large armfuls of papers and jam them into the plastic garbage pail in the corner of the room that served as a wastepaper basket.

"Will you marry me?" she asked.

"Not today," he said. "Today I've got to get a haircut. Anyway, I thought you girls didn't believe in marriage. No more nuclear families. Zero population growth. All that."

"See. There you go again. 'You girls.' Talking about us as a group. All women are to you are sex symbols. It's not right you know. You're as counterproductive as the bitch. You missed a piece under the bed." She sat back, bare-assed, on the desk, and lifted her feet out of Remo's way.

Remo leaned down and got the piece of paper out from the carpet of dust under the bed. "Where would the dirty, counterproductive bitch be in New York?"

"I don't know," the roommate said. "She said something stupid."

"What was that?"

"She said, watch out for the dead animals. And she was giggling. I think the bitch was on the nose candy again."

"Oh, the bitch."

"The dirty bitch."

"Oh, the dirty bitch," Remo agreed. "If I got my hands on her, I'd teach her a thing or two."

"You would?"

"You bet."

"Well, she belongs to this group. I bet you could find her there."

"What kind of group?"

"It's some kind of counterproductive revolutionary group. It would have to be counterproductive to have Joan Hackett in it."

"What's the name of it?" Remo asked.

"People United to Fight Fascism."

"Don't tell me," Remo said. "They call it PUFF."

"That's right."

"Where is it?"

"Someplace in the Village, but exactly where I don't know."

"What's your name?" Remo asked.

"Millicent Van Dervander."

"Of the dog food Van Dervanders?"

"Yes."

"I'll never look at a dog biscuit again without thinking of you."

"You're too kind."

"It's my basic nature," Remo said. "Listen, if I get time after my hair cut, you still want to get married?"

"No. You already have the room clean. Why get married?"

"Why indeed?"

Back at their room in the Hotel Guild, Chiun sat watching the last of his television shows.

"Come on, Chiun, we're going back to New York."

"Why?" Chiun said. "This is a very nice town. A place where you and I could settle down. And the hotel has cable television and I get many more channels than we do in New York City."

"We'll come back when they pave Garden Street," Remo said. "Anyway, New York City is very near to Brooklyn."

"Brooklyn is not all that important now," Chiun said sadly. "There are other things."

"Such as?"

"Such as the dead animals."

"Of course," Remo said. "I forgot. The dead animals. But you forgot the PUFF."

"The PUFF?"

"Yes," Remo said, "didn't you know. That comes before the dead animals. First fat, then thin, then PUFF, then the dead animals." He turned away with a malicious grin.

Chiun sighed behind him. "Let us go to Brooklyn," he said.

CHAPTER THIRTEEN

Back in New York, finding PUFF was not so easy as Remo had expected it to be. There was no reference to it in the files of the *New York Times,* no hand-printed sign on the main bulletin board of the New School for Social Research, not even a mention in the classified persons of the *Village Voice,* the *East Village Other* or *Screw Magazine.*

Finally, Remo gave up. After wasting the better part of a day, he called the special number.

"Smith here, is that you, Remo?"

"If you'd wait a minute, I'd tell you who was calling. You feeling all right?"

"Yes, yes," said Smith impatiently. "What have you found out?"

"Nothing. But I need some information. Do you have anything in those damned computers on an organization called PUFF?"

"PUFF? Like in magic dragon?"

"Yes, PUFF. People United to Fight Fascism or Freedom or some damn thing or other."

"Hold on."

Through the open phone, Remo could hear Smith mumbling, and then moments later, the clattering whoosh as the computer printout on his desk was activated.

Then Smith was back on the line.

"PUFF," he read. "People United to Fight Fascism. A lunatic fringe revolutionary group. Only several dozen members, mostly student children of rich parents. No known officers, no regular meeting dates. Last meeting was held six weeks ago in empty room over The Bard, a cocktail lounge on Ninth Street in the Village." He stopped reading and asked, "Why do you want to know this?"

"I'm thinking of joining," Remo said. "I hear the dues are tax deductible." He hung up before Smith pressed the point; Remo did not want him blundering around with more men and getting in his way.

After Remo had hung up, Smith spun around and looked out at the Sound. Smart-ass Remo would never understand. The conference on antiterrorist accords was to be held in three more days. The pressure was mounting. Despite all Chiun's nonsense about typhoons, suppose the hijackers struck again? Suppose there were other terrorist acts? The President himself was on the telephone every day, needling Smith about the lack of action. The pressure was building, building, building. Well, Dr. Smith knew how to handle pressure. He had handled it all his life. PUFF, eh? Smith wheeled back to his desk and began to jot notes down on a pad, notes that would send CURE's far-flung apparatus into operation against this organization called PUFF. It must be dangerous. He would flood the field with men. It might be a link to the terrorists. Let Remo be a smart-ass. "I hear dues are tax deductible." Oh, yes. Let him be as smart as he wanted. When Dr. Smith resolved the whole problem through CURE's other resources, then perhaps Mr. Remo Williams would see that he wasn't all that irreplaceable. And if he didn't see that, well, then, perhaps the point would have to be made more strongly.

With a slight smirk that looked ill at ease on Smith's drawn and dry face, he jabbed the point of his pencil down into the yellow pad, punctuating his anger with Remo, with CURE, with the President, with his country. But most of all, with Remo.

The object of all this indignation was, by then, on his way through the door of the lush cooperative apartment that CURE kept on the lower East Side of New York, Chiun trailing along in his wake.

"Is it?" Chiun asked.

"It is," Remo said.

"A visit to Brooklyn?"

"No," Remo said. "A lead on that Hacker girl."

"Oh, that," Chiun said. "Must we?"

"Yes, we must. Chiun, I promise you. A solid gold promise. When we're done, when we've got some time, we'll get to Brooklyn and see Barbra Streisand's house."

"Her ancestral home," Chiun corrected.

"Her ancestral home," Remo agreed.

"That solid gold promise could be tin," Chiun said.

"Why?"

"You may not be around to fulfill it. And then, what would happen to the promise? What would happen to me? Is it really likely that Dr. Smith would drive me to Brooklyn?"

"Chiun. For your sake, I'll try to live."

"One can but hope," Chiun said, quietly closing the door behind him.

The Bard was a noisy bar and restaurant, in a narrow side street near one of the Village's main drags. It was crowded and smoky when Remo and Chiun entered and the smoke was not all latakia. Chiun coughed loudly.

Remo ignored him and led the way to a table in the back corner from which he could watch the street outside, and also keep an eye on any people entering or leaving the bar.

Chiun sat down on the hard wooden bench facing Remo. "It is obvious that you do not care enough about my fragile lungs not to bring me here. But at least open a window for me."

"But the air conditioning's on," Remo protested.

"Yes. And it pumps into the air minute quantities of freon and ammonia gas that rob the brain of its will to resist. The air of the street is better. Even this street."

Remo looked at the window. "Sorry. These windows don't open."

"I see," Chiun said. "So that is the way it is to be." He turned to look at the window, all small panes set into steel frames, and nodded. "I see," he said again, and even though Remo knew what was coming, he could not react fast enough to do or say anything to stop Chiun's hand from flashing out, and pronging a steel-hard index finger against the corner of a window, neatly blasting out a piece of the wired glass, almost an inch square. The piece of glass fell outside with a muted tinkle and Chiun, now feeling very satisfied with himself, slid across the wooden bench and put his face close to the hole in the window and breathed deeply.

He turned back to Remo. "I found a way to open it."

"Yes, I see that. Congratulations."

Chiun held up a hand. "Think nothing of it."

Then the waitress was at their table, young, dark-haired, pretty, mini-skirted, and more interested in who they were and what they were doing there than in taking their order.

"We're Cheech and Chong doing field research," Remo said.

"Yeah," she said, twisting her gum inside her mouth, "and I'm Shirley MacLaine."

Chiun turned and squinted at her. "No, you are not Shirley MacLaine," he said, shaking his head with finality. "I saw her on the magic box, and you lack both her manners and her simplicity."

"Hey, watch it," the waitress said.

"What he meant was," Remo said, "that you're obviously a much more complex personality than Shirley MacLaine and that you don't waste time in those ritualistic niceties like doing ballets with good manners, but instead you let it all hang out in a symphony of truth and forthrightness."

"I do?"

"Yes," Remo said. "We noticed that as soon as we came in." He smiled at the girl and asked, "Now, what kind of juice do you have in the kitchen?"

She smi_ d back. "Orange, grapefruit, lemon, lime, tomato, carrot and celery."

"Would you mix us up large glasses of carrot and celery juice?" Remo asked.

"Macrobiotic, huh?"

Chiun looked pained. "Yeah," Remo said. "The latest thing. Mixed together, they let you think in the dark."

"Hey, wow," she said.

"And no ice," Remo said.

"You got it."

When she had left, Remo upbraided Chiun. "Now I told you we'll go to Brooklyn when we're done. You've got to be a little more civil."

"I will try to live up to your nation's high cultural standards, and not let it all hang out in a symphony of truth and forthrightness."

But Remo was no longer paying attention. His eyes were on a group of four who had just entered The Bard and were moving quickly through the dining area, alongside the bar, and then into a passageway that led somewhere into the back of the buiding. The first three were nondescript bomb-thrower types, a typical enough sight in the Village. Actually, so was the fourth, but with a difference. She was Joan Hacker. She wore tight jeans and a thin white sweater, a large floppy red hat and a black leather shoulder bag. She looked determined as she marched ahead behind the three men. Chiun turned and followed Remo's eyes.

"So that is the one?"

"Yes."

Chiun looked and said, "Be wary of her."

The girl had gone now into the back and Remo looked at Chiun questioningly. "Why? She's just a nit."

"All empty vessels are the same," Chiun said. "But some have milk poured into them and some poison."

"Thank you," Remo said. "That makes everything clear."

"You're welcome," Chiun said. "I am happy I was able to help. Anyway, just be careful."

Remo was careful.

He was careful until the waitress had brought back their juice, and careful to ask directions to the men's room which he knew was in the back, and careful that no one was looking when he got into the corridor, then darted up a flight of stairs.

He was careful at the top of the steps to stay outside the door and careful not to miss a word Joan Hacker said, or a gesture she made.

This was made immeasurably easier because none of the geniuses of the impending revolution had bothered to close the door to their meeting room and Remo could see clearly through the crack.

There were a dozen of them, all squatting on the floor, eight men and four women, and the only one standing was Joan Hacker. Their attention was riveted on her, as if she were Moses carrying the tablets down from the mountain. Remo could tell by looking at her that she gloried in the attention paid her; at Patton College, no one had listened to her, but here she was a very important person indeed.

"Now you all know what the plan is," she said. "No deviation will be allowed from it. It has been worked out on the highest levels . . . the very highest levels of the revolutionary movement. If we all do our part, it will not fail. And when the history of the Third World's rise is written, your names will loom large among those who were the makers of history."

Those, God help him, Remo thought, were her exact words. She seemed a little unsure delivering them, and he realized immediately why. They were someone else's words that she had memorized and was now reciting.

"I've got a question," a young woman said from the floor. She was skinny and buck-toothed and wore a too-large white sweater.

"Questions are allowed in our new order," Joan said.

"Why Teterboro?" the girl asked. "Why not Kennedy or LaGuardia?"

"Because we are walking before we run. Because we must show our strength. Because we were told to," Joan responded.

"But why?"

"Because," Joan shrieked. "That's why. And questions are counter productive. You either are or you aren't. You either do or you don't. I don't like questions. Our leaders don't like questions. All my life, people are always asking me questions, and well, I'm not going to answer them any more because what's right is right, whether you understand it or not." Her face was livid. She stamped her foot.

"She's right," one man said. "Questions are counter productive," thereby proving that he would rather bang Joan than the girl with buck teeth.

"Counter productive," another voice called. "Yes, down with counter productivity," came another.

Joan Hacker beamed. "Now that we're all agreed," and she underscored *all*, "let us proceed with our revolutionary fervor to do what must be done in the never-ending fight against fascism."

There was a collective nod of agreement from the audience and they began rising to their feet. Remo moved back slightly from the doorway to assure that he would not be glimpsed.

The thirteen people in the room milled around, everyone trying to talk at once, and Remo retreated downstairs, after first assuring himself that there was no other exit from the room.

As Remo reentered the dining section of The Bard,

he saw Chiun spot him in the mirror. Chiun immediately leaned over toward the window, and when Remo arrived at the booth, Chiun had his nose near the small hole in the glass. He was gasping as if he were a fish.

Remo, who knew that Chiun could live for a year inside a barrel of pickles without drawing a breath, said, "You know what you're breathing? Pizza crust and raw clams and baclava."

Chiun recoiled from the window. "Baclava?" he said.

"Yes," Remo said, "baclava. You start out by grinding these almonds and dates into a paste. Then you get a big pot of honey and gobs and gobs of sugar and. . . ."

"Hold. Enough," Chiun said. "I will take my chances in here."

Remo looked up and saw the first people from the meeting beginning to leave. He perched on the edge of his bench, ready to move when he saw Joan. She arrived three minutes later, the last of the group, and he got up and intercepted her in the doorway.

"You're under arrest," he whispered in her ear and when she turned, startled, and recognized him, he smiled.

"Oh, it's you," she said. "What are you doing here?"

"I'm on special assignment for the Patton College library."

She giggled. "I really ripped them off, didn't I?"

"Yes. And if you don't have a drink with me, I'm going to run you in."

"All right," she said, again the revolutionary leader. "But only because I want to. Because I'm supposed to tell you something and I'm trying to remember what it is."

He led her back to the table and introduced her to Chiun, who turned a withered smile in her direction.

"Excuse me for not arising," he said, "but I lack the strength. Was that polite enough, Remo?"

Joan nodded graciously to the old man, wondering for a moment what Remo was doing with the representative of the Third World and wondering if Chiun were Chinese or Vietnamese, and then abandoning the wonder as unworthy of a revolutionary leader.

"What are you drinking?" Joan asked Remo.

"A Singapore Sling," Remo said. "The latest thing in health drinks. Like one?"

"Sure, but not if it's too sweet. I've got this terrible toothache."

Remo called the waitress, motioned for her to refill his and Chiun's glasses, and said, "And another Singapore Sling for Madame Chiang here. And not too sweet."

"Still pretty sure of yourself, aren't you?" Joan Hacker asked, leaning forward and setting her bosom down onto the table top.

"No more than I have to be. Have you picked your targets yet?"

"Targets?"

"Targets. The bridges you're going to blow. Isn't that why you left school? To come down here and blow up the bridges? Paralyze New York. Seal it off from the rest of the country. Then direct the Third World revolution that will topple it from within?"

"If we hadn't had such a meaningful relationship,"

117

she said, "I'd think you were being sarcastic. Even if it isn't a bad idea."

"It's yours," Remo said, "to use as you will. You don't even have to give me credit for it. Only one proviso."

"Oh?"

"You have to leave the Brooklyn Bridge."

"Why?" she asked suspiciously, her mind already made up that if one were to blow up bridges around New York, the only one really worth blowing up would be the Brooklyn Bridge.

"Because Hart Crane wrote a great poem about it, and because people sometimes have important reasons to get to Brooklyn."

"Yes, indeed," Chiun said, removing his face from the hole in the window long enough to speak.

"All right," said Joan. "The bridge is yours." Quietly, she vowed to herself that the Brooklyn Bridge would be the first to go, meaningful relationship or no meaningful relationship.

"Can I charge tolls?" Remo asked, as the waitress put their drinks in front of them.

"Tolls will be outlawed in our new world," Joan said. "The bridges will belong to everybody."

"Good reason then to blow them up," Remo said. He lifted his glass and drained it. "Bottoms up," he said. Joan drained her drink.

"*Phewww,*" she said. "It's too sweet."

"I'll fix that," Remo said. "You'll see." He signaled the waitress for a refill for him and for Joan. "And not so sweet," he called.

Chiun still dawdled over his glass of juice.

Teterboro was what Joan had been talking about.

It was an airport in New Jersey and Remo had to find out what had been planned.

As she was halfway through her second drink, he broached the subject.

"I was only joking about the bridges," he said. "But if I were you guys, I'd really be doing something like that. You know, working on the transportation angle Imagine, tying up Kennedy Airport or bombing the runways at Newark Airport."

Joan Hacker giggled. "Child's play," she said.

"Child's play?" Remo said. "Not at all. It would be tough and dangerous and would really advance the cause of revolution. I think it's brilliant."

She slurped her glass until she had drained the last drop of heavy liquor from the bottom. Remo signaled for another as she said thickly, "You'll never be a revol-ara-lutionary. You don't think well enough."

"No? Well, you tell me a better idea."

"I will. How about if you took over the control tower? And had all the planes bumping into each other? Hah? Hah? Hah? Less work. More chaos. Terrific."

Remo shook his head in admiration. "Terrific," he agreed. "I've got to hand it to you. Sneak in after dark, say at midnight, take over the tower and whammo, instant chaos. Doubly so, during the nighttime."

She drained a big swig of her third Singapore Sling.

"Midnight, phooey," she said. "How about high noon? Daylight makes terror even more unbearable."

Chiun's ears perked up when he heard that. He turned from the window. "That is true, child. That is true. So it is written."

"You bet your sweet banana, so it's written," Joan Hacker confided to the Master of Sinanju, draining another swallow of her drink. "I know, for a fact. I have sources in the Third World too, you know."

She drank again.

"Oh, yeah," she said brightly to Remo. "Now I remember what I was supposed to tell you." She held her glass up over her head, letting the last drops roll into her mouth.

"What was that?" Remo said.

"I remember now," she said. "The dead animals are next."

Chiun turned slowly in his seat.

"I know that," Remo said. "Who told you to tell me?"

She rubbed her fingers together in the shame-shame gesture. "I'm not telling, I'm not telling, I'm not telling," Joan Hacker said, and then the revolutionary priestess smiled once, rolled her eyes back in her head and collapsed face forward on the table, unconscious.

Remo looked at her, then at Chiun, who stared at the drunken girl, shaking his head.

"There we are, Chiun, those dead animals again. Are you going to tell me what it's all about?"

"It will not matter," Chiun said. He looked at Joan again and shook his head.

"She is very young to die," he said.

"Everyone is very young to die," Remo said.

"Yes," Chiun said. "That is true. Even you."

CHAPTER FOURTEEN

Remo sensed the tail after he and Chiun had gone about two blocks from The Bard where Joan Hacker, high priestess of the impending revolution, slept on a table, the result of three Singapore Slings in fifteen minutes.

Remo motioned Chiun to stand with him and look into the window of a souvenir shop.

"Why am I forced to feign interest in all this Chinese shlock?" Chiun asked, using another of the Yiddish words he had learned on vacation a few years before.

"Quiet. We're being followed."

"Oh, my goodness," Chiun mocked. "By whom? Should I run? Should I scream for the police?"

"By that guy back there in the blue suit," Remo said. "Don't look now."

"Oh, my, Remo, you *are* wonderful. First for discovering him, and then for instructing me not to alert him that we have discovered him. How lucky I am to be allowed to accompany you." Chiun began to babble then, streams of Korean words, punctuated by an occasional in-English "how wonderful" or "how lucky I am."

Finally, it all dawned on Remo and he said sheepishly: "I guess you spotted him, too."

"The Master cannot lie," Chiun said. "I absorbed his vibrations. And also those of the other man who waits for us farther down the street and has been keeping one-half block ahead of us since we left that opium den."

"Where?" Remo said.

"Don't look now," Chiun said, giggling. "Oh, how lucky I am to be with you. Oh, how wonderful you are. Oh, how grand. Oh, how . . ."

"All right, Chiun, knock it off, will you? Anybody can make a mistake."

Chiun turned immediately serious. "But not one who presumes to challenge the dead animals. For him, any mistake will be his last. You are lucky again, however; these men are not the agents of the legend. You have nothing to fear."

That relieved the threat, but it did not answer the question: who were the men and why were they following Remo and Chiun?

The two men continued their tail, one behind and one ahead, as Remo and Chiun strolled casually back to their apartment, and Remo explained what the terrorists had planned for tomorrow. Teterboro was a small private airport in New Jersey, but probably one of the busiest airports in the world. Planes took off and landed every thirty or forty seconds. Seizing the control tower and giving conflicting traffic directions to different planes might touch off a chain reaction of accidents that could cost lives and create chaos.

And planes that would be frightened away by the accidents would probably wander into Newark Airport or Kennedy or LaGuardia, where their potential for accidental destruction would be fantastic, considering the big jet jobs coming in and out all the time.

"Why is it," Remo asked, "that no matter what terrorists are for, they always wind up killing people?"

Chiun shrugged unconcernedly. "It is a nothing."

"Dozens could die," Remo said heatedly.

"No," Chiun insisted. "There is an old Korean proverb. When two dogs attack, one barks but the other bites. Why do you spend your life worrying about barking dogs?"

"Yeah? Well, there's an old American proverb too," Remo said.

"I'm sure you will tell me of it."

"I will," Remo said, but did not since he was not able to think of one right offhand.

They continued walking in silence and in the middle of the next block, Remo said brightly:

"How about 'a stitch in time saves nine'?"

"I prefer 'haste makes waste,'" Chiun said.

"How about 'an ounce of prevention is worth a pound of cure'?" Remo offered.

"I prefer 'fools rush in where angels fear to tread,'" Chiun said.

"How about rice for supper tonight?" said Remo, restraining his impulse to strangle Chiun.

"Rice is nice," Chiun said sweetly, "but I prefer duck."

When they reached their apartment building, Remo sent Chiun upstairs with cautionary words not to kill either of the men who might try to follow him. Then Remo went around the corner, dallied long enough to be sure the tail had picked him up, and ducked into a dark cocktail lounge. He stood alongside the cigarette machine in the dimly illuminated foyer and waited. Seconds later, one of the tails came through the door. It was the one in the blue suit; the one who had trailed them from behind.

He blinked, trying to accustom his sun-shrunk eyes to the darkness, and Remo reached out and dug his right fingers into the man's left forearm.

"All right, pal," Remo said. "Who are you?"

The man looked up at Remo, his face a picture of innocence under his soft-brimmed felt hat, his body soft under his blue suit, and Remo knew. With a sinking feeling in the pit of his stomach, he knew where the man had come from.

The man inhaled. "Maher. IRS," he said. "If you let go of my arm, I'll show you my identification."

"That's all right," Remo said. "Why are you following me?" He squeezed the arm again to guarantee truth.

The man winced. "Don't know. Office assignment. Find out where you were going. Big deal. Mr. F.G. Maher. A field assignment, when all I am is an analyst."

"And your partner out there? Who's he?" Remo asked.

"That's Kirk. He's in my office."

"All right," Remo said, releasing the man. "Why not just go back and file your report that we went to the apartment building and that was that? We're not going out tonight. I promise you, so you can go home."

"Suits me," Maher said. "Tonight's the night Carolynn makes spaghetti and sausage."

"If you say one more word," Remo said, remembering the long-ago taste of it, "I'll kill you. Go away now."

Maher turned and left. Remo waited a few minutes and then went out onto the street and headed back toward his apartment building. Up ahead, he saw

124

Maher and his partner walking away from the building.

Goddam that Smith. The two men were obviously CURE agents. Just two more faceless dummies in the nationwide network of information-gathering that Smith had set up. Two more men who filed reports without any knowledge of to whom they really went.

Smith couldn't wait again. He was blundering around, sending in men, getting in Remo's way.

Remo got upstairs, picked up the telephone and dialed the 800 area-code number that rang on Smith's desk, ready to tell him just what he thought of him.

But the telephone rang and rang and for the first time that Remo could remember, there was no answer.

The next morning, Chiun refused to go with Remo to Teterboro. He was smugly adamant. "I will not expend my small store of energy on barking dogs," he said.

"Well, then, expend your energy watching Julia Child and try to learn to cook something someone can eat," Remo said, beating a hasty retreat.

In his rented car on the way to Teterboro, Remo thought of Chiun and his arrogant refusal to take the attack on Teterboro seriously. Lives were at stake, and another victory for the terrorists might screw up totally the antiterrorist agreement that was in the works.

Dammit, Teterboro was important, no matter what silly proverb Chiun came up with at any given moment.

That hijacked plane to Egypt had been important and so had the skyjacking over California. Any terrorist activity now was important, when the nations of the world were so close to working out an agreement to cut down terrorists in their tracks. Chiun just didn't understand.

Remo knew that he, himself, didn't hold out too much hope for the antiterrorist pact ever being the panacea that Smith seemed to think it was. Still, that was a decision for Remo's government to make. It was his job to try to see that the agreement was carried out.

Teterboro was tucked away in suburban New Jersey, only minutes from Manhattan.

Remo pulled into a parking spot alongside the fence that separated the hangars from a small side street, and walked through an opening in the fence onto the field. There were no guards, no security, no one to ask him who he was and what he was doing there. The airport was made for ripping off.

Remo was walking toward the control tower when he saw it. A Red Cross wagon was parked near the tower, its side doors only ten feet from the entrance to the tower.

A stakeout. Someone inside watching. But who? Friend or foe, Remo wondered, afraid that he already knew the answer.

He darted into a hangar, and moved through it, then into another hangar, and another, and finally exited somewhere behind the Red Cross truck. From the shadows, he looked the truck over carefully. The windows were extremely shiny glass, obviously one-way mirrors and he could see no one in the cab. Casually, he strolled up to the side of the wagon and pounded on the two closed doors.

"What do you want?" came the lemony, puckered voice that Remo had come to know and hate.

"I'm new in town," Remo yelled, "and I want my brochure on local places of interest."

"Go see your Chamber of Commerce," came back Dr. Smith's voice, muffled by the closed doors.

"I will not. This is a welcome wagon, isn't it? Well, you just come out of there and welcome me to town." He pounded again. Inside he heard the shuffling of steps. He continued to pound.

Finally the door opened a crack. Dr. Harold W. Smith's beady eyes peered out, saw Remo, and did a doubletake.

"It's you," he said.

"Of course," Remo said. "Who did you expect? The Man from Glad?"

"Well, come in," Smith said distastefully, "and stop that bellowing out there." Remo shared the feeling of distaste; Smith was interfering again.

Remo moved into the small van. There were three other men there besides Smith and they were carefully scanning the field in all directions. They did not even bother to turn their heads to look at Remo.

Smith pulled Remo toward the back of the wagon and said, "How'd you get here?"

"I drove."

"I mean, how did you find out?"

"Oh. From the people at PUFF. They're involved in it, you know."

"Yes, I know," Smith said.

His voice oozed disgust and Remo said, "You're not really sore that I'm here, are you? I can just as soon leave."

"No. As long as you're here, stay and watch. Maybe

you'll learn something about how a professional operates," Smith said.

"How'd you find out about it?" Remo asked. "One of them talk?"

"Yeah. Some skinny little thing with buck teeth. She was only too glad to talk. She thought the whole idea was stupid. Where is Chiun, by the way?"

"He's back in New York," Remo said. "I think he's working up a new supply of proverbs for next week."

"Proverbs?" Smith asked offhandedly, his attention fixed on a pile of papers on a small table in front of him.

"Yeah, you know, things like 'when two dogs attack, one barks, but the other bites.' "

"Dogs?" said Smith, not paying attention, resenting any distraction from the numbers he was reading on a long yellow pad.

"Yes. Dogs. You know, ungrateful curs. Bite the hand that feeds them. Carriers of dirt and disease. Rabies spreaders. Dogs."

"Yes," Smith said. "Hmmm, that's right. Dogs."

One of the men in the front of the van called, "Mr. Jones! They're coming!"

Smith wheeled and ran to the front of the van. Remo shook his head. Jones, he thought. What an original alias.

"How many are there?" he heard Smith ask.

"Six of them," the man replied, his face still pressed to the darkened one-way window. His voice had that flat Midwestern label that FBI agents wear. "Five men and a girl."

"I want to see the girl," Remo said, walking to the front of the cab.

"You would," Smith snarled.

Remo looked between Smith and the agent and saw the six hippie types approaching. He recognized the girl from yesterday's PUFF meeting, but was disappointed that it wasn't Joan Hacker. It was time to wring the truth out of her.

They came closer now to the tower, skulking in the high-noon daylight, their attempts at being inconspicuous making them look like a marching band.

The three FBI men moved away from their windows and took up positions alongside the twin doors of the Red Cross van.

Smith watched the group from the window. "Be alert, men," he hissed. "When I tell you, open the doors, jump out and collar them."

Remo shook his head. Stupid. The place for the agents to be was inside the control tower, to cut off the six hippies. Suppose one got loose and got inside? Remo shook his head again.

"Okay, men, on your toes now," Smith said.

"Ready?" He paused. "Okay. Now!"

The three agents flung open the doors and jumped out onto the black asphalt. "Federal Bureau of Investigation," one called. "You're under arrest."

The six hippies turned—shocked, and then five reluctantly raised their hands. But the sixth ran through the door of the control tower, heading for the flight of stairs. With a bound, Remo was out of the cab, through the agents and their captives, and then inside the control tower.

The youth who had bolted had a gun and he

129

pegged a shot at Remo on the narrow stairwell leading up to the nerve center of the tower.

Remo made it miss and then was on the youth who never had a chance to fire another shot.

"All right, Fidel," he said. "The war's over."

He collared the youth by the neck and beard and began to drag him down the stairs. Just as he shoved him outdoors into the bright summer sunshine, the youth began to laugh. Loud. Uproariously. Eyewetting gales of laughter.

"What's the joke?" Remo asked. "Let us all in on it."

"You think you have caught someone," the youth said through his laughing. "But the revolution will go on. You have caught the barking dog. And now, another shall bite."

Inspiration. Suddenly, Remo realized what Chiun had meant. Remo and Smith were here, wasting their time on a harmless dog. But there was another dog out there, somewhere, with teeth, and he was about to bite.

"Smitty," Remo yelled. "Quick."

Smith looked pained that Remo had blown his cover name of Jones, and even more pained when Remo grabbed him by the arm and pulled him to the back of the van, away from the ears of the curious FBI agents. "Quick. Is there something else going on today? Something to do with the terrorist pact?"

Smith hesitated and Remo said, "Hurry, man, or you're going to have a disaster on your hands."

"The three officers who are working out the agreement are meeting secretly today in New York," Smith

130

said. "Finishing it up for tomorrow's meeting at the U.N."

"Where are they meeting?"

"At the Hotel Caribou."

"What time?" Remo asked.

Smith glanced at his watch. "Just about now," he said. "Room 2412 at the Caribou."

"Does this thing have a phone?" Remo asked, nodding toward the van.

"Yes, but . . ."

Remo jumped into the van, got a mobile operator and called his apartment. The phone rang. And rang. And rang. Please, Chiun, be in a good mood. Don't break the instrument in half because someone dares interrupt "As the Planet Revolves." Please, Chiun, answer.

Finally, the phone stopped ringing. Agonizingly slowly, it was being raised to an ear. Another pause and then Remo could hear Chiun's voice, mocking him, and he could picture the look in Chiun's eyes as the old man said into the phone:

"Where is the dog that bites?"

CHAPTER FIFTEEN

The Hotel Caribou was only a few blocks from their apartment. Remo told Chiun to protect at all costs the lives of the three men meeting in Room 2412.

Then he burned up the highway in his rented car, hoping to meet Chiun at the hotel before anything happened.

Remo was too late.

When he pulled up to the Caribou and double-parked out in the street, police cars already were pulling in at angles before the main entrance.

Remo sidled into the crowd of police and detectives and asked, "What happened?"

"Don't know," one policeman said. "Three people killed somehow."

So Chiun had been too late. He had not been able to get to the Caribou on time. And because Remo would not listen or try to understand the proverb about the dogs, and because he arrogantly had gone ahead to Teterboro Airport, the three colonels were dead and the antiterrorist pact set back for, only God knew, how long a period of time.

Stupid, stupid, stupid, Remo accused himself as he ducked into the hotel and started up to the twenty-fourth floor to see if there were any pieces that he could pick up to try to salvage something.

Clever, clever, clever.

It had really been well done, the old man told

himself as he walked slowly down the street, back to the East Side apartment.

The assassination attempt had been clever, but its planner should have known that it would not deceive the Master of Sinanju. Perhaps, Chiun thought, someone thinks that Chiun is growing too old. That he has lost his skills. Fool, he thought.

All his life, he had been sustained in his work by his pride in his skills; and then, one day, the use of them had become an end in itself, as it had, he was sure, with every Master of Sinanju who had come before him.

Now Chiun used his skills, and the poor and the young of his village lived. It was that simple. Life was always simple for those who did not try to get out of it more than was in it.

Still, he mused, it would be nice to retire. To sit back in the village of Sinanju, at the edge of the water, mending fish nets, children about him, paying to him the respect and homage that was due a Master who had gone out into the world beyond the seas and had come back with victory over all the world's challenges.

But before that could happen, there would have to be a Master to replace him. And of course that meant Remo, who could not really be a white man. Somewhere in the mongrel matings that produced all Americans, there must have been a Korean, blood of Chiun's blood, a member of the House. Remo was too good to be just a white man.

It had been Chiun's plan from the first moment he had met the young American. The American had looked at him, down the barrel of a gun, and with no qualms, no misgivings, no second thoughts, had attempted to shoot Chiun. That had been ten years ago, and in those ten years, a mere ten years, Remo had advanced his skills almost to the point of perfection. Chiun thought with pride of Remo's genius, his ability to do things with his body that before him, only Chiun in the world could do.

Only Chiun and one other.

One other. Remo had come far, but now he faced grave danger. It was in his nature to scoff at the tales of typhoons and of dead animals and of the dog who bites, but there was more truth to legends than to history; history tells only of the past, but legends tell of the past and present and future.

So, while Remo might laugh in his vile American way, he must be protected from the mortal threat of the dead animals, no matter whether he wished to be or not. This was Chiun's commitment to the people of Sinanju, who looked to their Master, not only for sustenance, but for the appointment of a new Master who would continue that sustenance.

And that someday Master was now in peril of his life. The episode today at the Hotel Caribou had shown that. It would have been normal to presume that the three men who were meeting inside Room 2412 would be attacked from outside. Remo might have made that presumption. But Chiun had found the three would-be assassins inside the room, cloaked in the garb of security men, there supposedly to protect the three colonels but actually assigned to kill them.

Well, they would kill no more. Chiun had seen to that, and then had removed the three important men to another room where they could be safe and could continue their meeting in privacy.

Yet, the plan of attack had been well-conceived. And those conceptions were drawing nearer and nearer to Remo, threatening him, and Chiun wished that Remo could be convinced to move away from this assignment. It was for that reason that Chiun had refused to tell Remo what the legends meant and who his adversary was. For, if once Remo knew, his pride would prohibit him from walking away. Instead, he would seek out his confrontation with the enemy. So, he kept Remo ignorant of the truth.

As he turned into the door of the apartment building, the tiny, aged Oriental smiled slightly to himself, recalling the look on the face of the Chinese officer when Chiun had entered the room and disposed of the three assassins. The look told of a man who had heard the legends, and had, at that very moment, come to believe them; the look of a man who knew he was seeing a typhoon blow.

And as the typhoon named Chiun rode up in the apartment house elevator, he vowed that if it must come to it, Remo would be protected from the dead animals, even at the cost of Chiun's own life. Even at the cost of breaking a lifelong vow that the Master of Sinanju would never raise hand against another from his village.

CHAPTER SIXTEEN

"All right, Chiun, how'd you do it?"

Chiun turned to look at Remo, who was pacing up and down the carpeted floor of the living room of their apartment.

"Do? Do what?"

"The three colonels. How did you know the security men were fakes?"

Chiun shrugged, his shoulders moving slightly underneath the heavy brocaded blue robe. "One knows what one knows," he said.

"All right, then, how did you know that the attack on Teterboro was a red herring?"

He looked at Chiun who was about to speak and said disgustedly, "I know, I know, 'one knows what one knows,'" parroting Chiun's Oriental sing-song. "But why the hell didn't you tell me?"

"But I did tell you. I warned you of the dog that barks and the dog that bites. If you then choose to join a chorus of barking dogs in baying at the moon, that is your business."

"You've got to stop talking to me in riddles, Chiun. I've got to know what things mean," Remo said.

"All things are riddles to him who will not think," Chiun said, folded his hands over his chest and turned from Remo to gaze out the window into smog-laden New York.

Remo exhaled an exasperated puff of air, started to speak again, but was interrupted by a knock upon the door. "Now what?" he mumbled to himself. "First fat, then thin, then the dead animals," he said, again parroting Chiun. "This is probably the dead animals."

"Come in, it's open," he roared.

The door pushed open and Dr. Harold W. Smith stood there. He looked with disgust at the open door, as if it had somehow offended him, then said, "I'm glad to see that you are still vitally concerned with your own security."

Remo had already this day had enough of Smith to last him the rest of his life. "What's to worry?" he asked jauntily. "Now that I know you're having us tailed, what do we have to fear? Have no fear, CURE is here."

"That was a mistake," Smith said. "We had agents following everyone who left The Bard. Two of them just happened to pick you up."

"And two of them damn near got killed for their trouble," Remo said. "Will you tell me why you are suddenly sticking your patrician nose into field business? Since when has it become necessary for you to chaperone me?"

"I might in turn ask, since when have you questioned my decisions on the correct way to handle things?" Smith said stiffly.

"Since you've been running around like a chicken with its head cut off," Remo said. "Look, if you had told me in advance that the colonels were meeting today, we would have protected it. But we didn't know. And so we almost bought the farm. But now, we do know that the formal conference at the U.N. is tomorrow. So why don't you just go back to Folcroft and count paper clips? Chiun and I will take care of the conference."

"How?" Smith asked drily. "When you don't even know what way an attack might come?"

"I'll tell you how," Remo said. "I'm going back after Joan Hacker this afternoon, and I'm going to squeeze her like a lemon until she talks. I should have done that before. And then we're going to wrap up this whole thing."

"Absolutely not," Smith exploded. "You are going to do precisely what I say and what I say is do not, *repeat do not,* go blundering around. You might force the terrorists into some unpredictable action that we will not be able to control."

"And you'll be able to control anything else, I suppose?" Remo said. "How? With those goddam computers?"

"If you must know, I expect that those goddam computers, as you call them, will have enough information for us tonight, to absolutely guarantee the safety of tomorrow's formal conference. We are questioning every one who was at the PUFF meeting at The Bard. Scraps of information, names, dates, relatives and friends. Our computer will decipher it for us."

Chiun, who had sat quietly through the argument, looked at Smith and shook his head sadly.

"A typhoon does not register on a computer," he said softly.

"Oh yes," Smith said. "You and all this nonsense. What is this business about a typhoon? What is this business about dead animals? I'm tired of hearing about them."

138

"They are legends, Dr. Smith, and that means they are true."

"Then what do they mean?"

"They mean that two typhoons may yet confront each other. They mean that the danger will come in the place of the dead animals."

"Typhoons? What two typhoons?" Smith snarled.

"Don't look to me for help," Remo said. "He won't tell me either." Chiun turned his back, indicating the lecture was over. Smith's face grew red with rage.

"Remo. You're off this case. I'm taking full control from now on in."

Remo shrugged. "Suit yourself," he said. He flopped back on the sofa, kicked off his loafers and began to leaf through a copy of *Gallery,* looking at the pictures. "Just be sure you do as good a job as you did today in protecting those three colonels," Remo said.

Angrily, Smith turned and left, slamming the door shut behind him.

"Poor Smith," Remo said aloud to himself. "He's gone off the deep end. Worrying about those paper clips and the cost of pencils and my expense account —it's finally all numbed his brain."

"No," Chiun corrected. "He is on the edge, but I see signs that he will be soon well again."

"Now how can you see that?"

"Never mind. I can see it," Chiun said. "Soon he will resume his life as if this period had never existed."

"Can't come too soon for me," Remo said. "He's nasty enough when he's well."

"In the meantime, however," Chiun said, "he has

relieved you of duty. May we not now just depart from this place to a place of clean air? Perhaps Brooklyn?"

"You don't really think, do you, Chiun, that I'd walk away from this assignment?"

"No," Chiun sighed. "I did not suppose you would. Loyalty often transcends common sense."

Some day, this loyalty would be given where it belonged, to the House of Sinanju, which made this white man into a pupil of Sinanju. Some day, there would be a new Master of Sinanju, if misplaced loyalty did not get him killed first.

CHAPTER SEVENTEEN

The waitress at The Bard remembered Remo. No, the girl who had conked out at his table had not been back. But the waitress would keep an eye out for her and if she could have Remo's phone number at home, why, she would be sure to call in case the girl showed up.

Next on the list was a phone call to Patton College to Millicent Van Dervander. Why, certainly, she remembered Remo.

"Are you coming back to Patton?"

"Why? Is your room dirty again?" he asked.

"No. But you and I could mess it up some."

Then followed the announcement that the bitch had not come back, but she had called. No, she didn't even apologize. All she had wanted was an address from the desk phone book she had left behind.

Whose address?

Let me look it up. It was the phone number of a dentist. She had lost a cap from her tooth. Millicent hoped the dentist would sew her mouth shut.

"Yes. Here it is. Dr. Max Kronkeits," and she gave Remo an address on the upper West Side.

Dr. Kronkeits' nurse was forty-two years old, had a tendency to weight, and liked to be home on time. She was just getting ready to leave when the young man showed up. He made it very clear that while the foolish world might have one opinion, his own personal opinion was that women should be substantial, not frail wispy things that threatened to evaporate when touched. Because, of course, women were made to be touched. Strangely enough, he conveyed all this information to her without saying a word, just by his look.

When he got around to saying a word, it was to ask about Joan Hacker. Miss Hacker, the nurse informed Remo, had called and was now on her way. Dr. Kronkeits was going to recap an upper right frontal bicuspid.

Remo explained to the nurse that he was from the FBI, that it was important that Joan Hacker not know that he had been asking for her, that when the case was over, Remo would come back and explain to the nurse, perhaps over a drink or two, just how it had worked out and how helpful the nurse had been. Of course, secrecy now was essential.

And so it was that Remo was waiting near the front door of the West Side apartment building in which Kronkeits had his office when Joan Hacker arrived. An hour later she came out, and Remo began following her on the other side of the street. She wore tight jeans and a thin, white, floppy blouse, and she smiled as she walked down the street. Remo noted this was the most common reaction of people who are putting distance between themselves and a dentist's office.

She walked along Central Park West for three blocks, Remo casually strolling along with her, pace for pace, then she turned into a street in the high eighties. She sauntered down the street, happily swinging her red shoulder bag, and then turned into a small coffee shop in mid-block.

When Remo entered the shop, Joan Hacker was sitting at a table in the back, anxiously drumming her fingertips on the red formica table top, glancing over her shoulder at a door in the rear.

She hardly noticed Remo when he sat down across from her.

"Back again," he said. "This time for some answers."

"Oh, you," she said. "Why don't you just leave me alone? I've got things to do."

"And I'm not going to let you do any of them," he said.

She stopped drumming on the table and met his eyes. "You are really a ridiculous reactionary," she said. "Do you actually think you can stop our glorious revolution?"

"If your glorious revolution means rape and baby killing, then I can try."

"You can't make an omelet without breaking the eggs," she said.

"Particularly when your brain is scrambled to begin with. Now some answers. What's going to happen tomorrow?"

"Tomorrow?" She laughed. "Tomorrow every one of those delegates to the antiterrorist convention is going to be killed. Every one." She seemed almost pleased to tell him. "Isn't that glorious?" she asked.

"Murder glorious?" he said.

"You know what you are?" she asked. "You're a dinosaur. A dinosaur." She giggled. "Plodding around in the past, trying to stop tomorrow. I just saw one. You're a dinosaur."

She was interrupted by a voice from the back of the room.

"You can come in now."

Remo looked up. The speaker was a young Puerto Rican. He wore the uniform of The Gauchos, a street group that had been set up as the Boriqueño equivalent of the Black Panthers, but which had pretty well died out when the TV networks stopped covering their antics. He wore a brown beret, a brown shirt with military patches and emblems, brown slacks tucked into highly polished paratrooper boots. The youth was small and slim, perhaps twenty, and he crooked an imperious finger at Joan, beckoning her to follow him.

She got up and turned to Remo again. "A dinosaur," she said. "And just like all the dinosaurs that couldn't accept change, you're going to be dead." Her voice was an angry hiss.

"I'm going to wait for you," Remo said. "Right here. We're not done talking yet."

She stomped away from him and went into the backroom. Remo went to the counter at the front of the shop, sat on the stool nearest the door, and ordered coffee.

But all hopes he had of hearing what went on behind the door were shattered as one of the customers put a quarter in the jukebox, and it began to blare out the music of a Latin band that sounded as if it had one hundred men on first trumpet.

Behind the door, Joan Hacker looked around the room, into the nut-brown faces of twenty-five young

Puerto Ricans, swallowed and explained what she wanted.

"Why you come to us?" one young man, with more medals and insignia than the others asked.

"Because we're told that you are tough and smart."

"Oh, yes," he said, with a toothy grin, "we are tough, girl. That is because we are men. The men of the streets. And we are smart too. We understand that is why you did not get Negritos for this work."

She nodded, even though she felt it was not proper for them to feel that way about blacks. After all, they were part of the same Third World. Perhaps if she had more time, she could have made them see that they and the black men were brothers. But she did not have the time.

Others around the room now were nodding, babbling. "Right. We smart. Not like the others." Another said, "Damn right, we men. Lady, you want us to show you how much man we are?" Many of them chuckled; Joan felt their eyes on her thinly clad bosom and wished she had worn a jacket.

The leader said: "Do you have the money?"

"I have half the money. The other half comes after," she said.

"And for this, we are to demonstrate at the United Nations tomorrow?"

"Yes," she said. "But no violence."

"That is much money, just to hold a parade," he said cautiously.

"There will be more, if your demonstration is big enough." Joan Hacker thought of Remo sitting outside. "There is one other thing," she said.

"What is this one other thing?" the leader asked.

145

When the door opened, Remo turned, expecting to see Joan Hacker. But again, the slim Puerto Rican was there. He looked around the room, his eyes lighted on Remo, and he said: "The girl wants you."

Remo hopped off the stool and followed the youth into the backroom. But inside, he saw that Joan Hacker had gone. There was a back door leading from the large meeting room. That door was now blockaded by ten youths. Remo felt a hand press between his shoulder blades and push. He allowed himself to be propelled forward into the middle of the floor. Behind him now were another dozen young men.

"Where's the girl?" Remo said, trying to sound inoffensive. "I thought you said she wanted to see me."

"When we are done with you," the young leader said, "no one will ever again want to see you."

He looked around the room. "Who wants him?"

There were shouts from both sides.

"You, Carlo," the leader said, and another youth, taller and huskier than the rest, stepped away from the rear door, his face split wide in a grin.

He reached into a back pocket and brought out a black-handled knife, then pressed the button and a six-inch blade snapped forward into place, glinting white and shiny under the overhead fluorescent lights.

He held the knife in front of him, holding it correctly, like the right hand on a golf club, and began to wave it back and forth in front of him.

"You want him in big pieces or little pieces, El Jefe?" he asked.

The leader laughed and while the others chuckled, he said: "Bite size chunks."

"Hold on a minute," Remo said. "Don't I get a knife too?"

"No."

"I thought you guys believed in fair fights. How fair a fight is it if I don't have a knife?"

"You want a knife?" said the youth known as El Jefe, "You shall have a knife." He snapped his fingers. "Juan. Your knife." A tiny youth, no older than sixteen, handed him a knife from his pocket. El Jefe snapped it open, looked at its long blade, then turned and slipped the blade in the crack between the door and the jamb. Then he wrenched the handle to the left, snapping off the blade and leaving only the handle.

He turned with a grin and tossed it to Remo. "Here, gringo. Here is your knife."

Remo plucked the handle out of the air. "Thanks," he said. "That'll do." He curled the knife into his right fist.

"Go get him, Carlo!" shouted El Jefe. "Cut the *marichon*."

Carlo jumped into the attack like a fencer. Remo stood his ground. Only three feet separated them now. Carlo waved his knife back and forth in the slow hypnotic movements of a cobra, following the snake charmer's flute.

Then he lunged. He aimed the knife point at Remo's solar plexus, and moved forward, knife, hand and arm. Remo moved aside, and as Carlo turned to cover, Remo's left hand darted out and flicked off the bottom of Carlo's right ear lobe.

"Lesson number one," Remo said. "Don't lunge. Slash."

There was a collective sip of air around the room. Carlo felt the blood trickle down his neck. He went wild, jumping forward toward Remo, his knife slashing air back and forth. But then Remo was behind him, and as Carlo turned to him, Remo put his left thumb into Carlo's cheekbone. The loud crack as the bone popped resounded through the room.

"Lesson number two," Remo said. "Don't take your eyes off the target."

Carlo now was frantic, rage fighting with fear for possession of his body. With a scream, he raised his knife over head and ran at Remo, planning to plunge it down into Remo's body.

Remo stood his ground, but then as Carlo reached him, Remo went up into the air. His right arm, which he had not thus far used, went up over his head, and then the hand came down on the top of Carlo's skull. The unbladed knife crashed against the top of Carlo's head, and then the pressure carried the handle through the bone, and the knife was imbedded deep in his brain. Carlo staggered once, then fell to the floor.

"Lesson number three," Remo said. "Don't screw around with me. I'm El Exigente, and I won't buy your beans."

He walked to the front door, and the twelve Puerto Ricans scattered to let him pass through. As he walked out, Remo grabbed El Jefe by the windpipe and dragged him along behind him.

In the street outside the coffee shop, El Jefe decided to tell Remo everything. The girl was obviously an idiot; she had agreed to pay two thousand dollars for The Gauchos to picket the United Nations tomorrow. No, they would not commit any violence. And no, if

Señor did not want them to show up, they would not even show up, because maintaining the social order was more important than money to them.

"Show up," Remo said, gave El Jefe's windpipe a squeeze of remembrance, and walked off down the street.

No point in looking for the girl; she had gotten away by now. But the main line tomorrow was to be an attack on the delegates; he and Chiun would be there to stop it.

CHAPTER EIGHTEEN

The streets were already speckled black with dots of people as the sun rose over the East River.

The United Nations building loomed cold and foreboding over the crowd, an architectural cigarette pack, but then the crowd warmed and came alive as the building's black wedge of shadow raced backwards along the streets to rejoin the base of the building.

The demonstrators were young—many blacks, many Puerto Ricans, but mostly white—all mindlessly carrying placards and signs.

YOU CAN'T OUTLAW LIBERTY.

WE'LL FIGHT FOR FREEDOM.

And yes, Remo saw one marked, PEOPLE UNITED TO FIGHT FASCISM, and he recognized the sign wielder as one of The Gauchos he had played with yesterday.

The antiterrorist conference was scheduled to begin at 11 A.M. The few people who would get the seats in the gallery had already been herded behind ropes near the building's main entrance. Still the mob of demonstrators continued to swell and surge out in front of the building in which men tried usually to keep peace in an unbalanced world, but today were to attempt the just-as-difficult task of outlawing hoodlumism on an international scale.

Remo turned from the television set in disgust as the demonstrators spotted a camera on them and broke into an organized chant:

Hey, hey, hey, hey.

People's wars won't go away.

Chiun smiled. "Something intrudes upon your sense of order?" he said.

"Sometimes it seems we spend all our time trying to protect our country. . . ."

"Your country," Chiun interjected.

"My country from nit-nats. The politicians won't let us build new jails, but how about one big asylum? That'd end most of our social problems."

"It would only start them," Chiun said. "I remember once, many years ago. . . ."

"No, Chiun, not again," Remo said. "I'm filled up to here with typhoons, and with fat, and thin and dead animals, and dogs that bark and dogs that bite, and I just don't need anymore."

"Have it your own way," Chiun said mildly, returning his gaze to the television. "I suppose we must go out there today in the midst of all those lowlifes."

"Yes," Remo said, "and we've got to leave soon. Somebody's going to make an assassination try on the delegates; we've got to stop it."

"I see you have not reconsidered your dismissal by Dr. Smith."

"We both know, Chiun, that *that* doesn't work. I'm in this for life, whether Smith likes it or not."

"A strange kind of loyalty in which one disobeys his employer?"

"My employer is the United States," Remo said, "not Dr. Harold W. Smith."

Chiun shrugged. "I must have slept through the referendum in which two hundred million people expressed their confidence in you."

151

"It wasn't necessary."

"Those two hundred million people do not even know you exist," Chiun said. "Dr. Smith does; he pays your salary; you report to him; therefore he is your employer."

"Have it your own way. After this is over, we'll file a complaint with the National Labor Relations Board." Remo tumbled into a one-hand hand-stand against the far wall, and called upside down to Chiun: "C'mon. We've got to limber up."

"You limber up. I will watch and make comments."

But Chiun was silent as Remo went through almost an hour of gymastics around the living room floor. Finally, he stopped and said: "Time to go. What makes it worse is that Smith is going to be skulking around, probably with six hundred agents. We've got to be careful we don't knock off any of his men."

"It will be easy," Chiun said. "Be on the lookout for the men wearing trench coats and carrying knives in their teeth." He allowed himself a smile, as he followed Remo to the door.

He watched Remo's smooth glide approach to the door, and again he worried. Not for himself, but for Remo because the force against them was powerful enough to kill the young American who would one day be Master of Sinanju. And Remo should recognize that force, but he did not. Yet, if Chiun should tell him, Remo's mistaken pride would force him to go onward, exposing himself to danger. As painful as it was, he must wait for Remo to find out himself.

"Do you never wonder who is behind all this terrorism?" Chiun asked Remo.

"I don't have to wonder," Remo said. "I know."

"Oh?"

"Yes," Remo said. "It's the dog who barks but sometimes bites, who will bite fat but prefers thin and who waits at the place of the dead animals for PUFF, the magic flagon."

"Let us hope he does not wait for you. Because while we protect these men today, nothing will be changed unless the one responsible for this is destroyed."

"That's next," Remo said.

Chiun shook his head sadly and moved into the doorway. "It can never be next. It must always be now."

Remo started to answer but was interrupted by the telephone behind him.

As Chiun waited at the doorway, Remo stepped back into the apartment to answer the call.

A girl's voice said, breathlessly, "Remo, you've got to come. This has all gotten out of hand."

"Joan," Remo said. "Where are you?"

"At the place of the dead animals. At the Mu . . ."

And the phone went dead.

Remo looked at the receiver for a moment, then slowly replaced it. It was the face-to-face he'd wanted. But where? And how? He turned to Chiun who saw the look of puzzlement on Remo's face, and said gently: "It will come to you. It has been planned that way."

Remo just stared at him.

On the other side and at the other end of town, Joan Hacker hung up the phone with a self-satisfied smile.

153

"How did I do?" she asked.

"Magnificently, my revolutionary flower." The man who spoke was small and yellow-skinned. His voice was even and placid.

"Then you think I fooled him?"

"No, my dear, of course you did not fool him. But that does not matter. He will come. He will come."

Remo and Chiun began the long walk uptown toward the United Nations Building. Remo tried to rebuild the girl's words in his mind; twice he bumped into people on the street; twice Chiun clucked disapprovingly.

They slowed down slightly as they heard the happy shouts of children playing in a playground. Remo turned to watch. A set of boy-girl twins were at the top of a large fiberglass slide. It was shaped like a brontosaurus, that biggest, fattest of prehistoric dinosaurs, and Remo noticed for the first time how perfectly its smooth sloping back had been designed for use as a slide. He smiled absently to himself, then looked again. Something about the shape of the slide; it was familiar; he had seen that shape in just that way before. Then it hit him—where Joan Hacker had called from, the place of the dead animals. And, for the first time, it also came to him who was behind the terrorists. Who it had to be.

He stopped and put his hand on Chiun's shoulder.

"Chiun," he said. "I know."

"And now you go?"

Remo nodded. "You have to go on and protect the delegates to the conference."

Chiun nodded. "As you will. But remember, care. Yours is the dog that bites; the ones I seek only bark."

Remo squeezed Chiun's shoulder and Chiun averted his eyes at the rare display of affection. "Don't worry, Little Father. I'll bring back victory in my teeth."

Chiun raised his eyes to meet Remo's. "The last time the two of you met, I told you he was five years better than you," Chiun said. "I was wrong. You are equal now."

"Only equal?" Remo asked.

"Equal may be good enough," Chiun said, "because he has fears that you do not have. Go, now."

Remo turned and moved away from Chiun, quickly, melting and disappearing into the early-morning workbound crowd. Chiun watched him go, then said a silent prayer to himself. There were so many things that Remo must yet learn, and yet one could not coddle the next Master of Sinanju.

Around the corner, Remo looked down the street. Every cab he saw had at least one head, and sometimes two in the back seat. Waiting for an empty might take forever.

He moved to the corner and when one cab slowed to pass workmen who were digging up the street, he grabbed the doorhandle, pulled the door open and slipped into the back seat, onto the lap of a young woman carrying a model's hatbag. She was beautiful, placid and serene and she said:

"Hey, creep. Wotsa mattuh witcha?"

"It's good to know your beauty's not just skin deep," Remo said, as he leaned across her, opened the door on her side, and pushed her out into the street.

He slammed the door again and said: "Museum of Natural History and step on it."

From the driver's seat, P. Worthington Rosenbaum started to protest. Then, in the rearview mirror, he caught a glimpse of Remo's eyes, and decided to say nothing.

Remo sat back and thought of the Museum, which he had last visited on a bus trip from the Newark orphanage where he'd grown up. The square blocks of buildings. The floor after floor of exhibits. The glass cases showing different forms of life in their native habitat. And the room where the dinosaurs were. The brontosaurus with the playground-slide back. Tyrannosaurus with his foot-long teeth. Exact skeletal reproductions of the animals as they had been when they lived.

Joan Hacker had tried to tell him yesterday when she told him he was a dinosaur. She had been trying to tip him, but he was too dumb to grasp it.

And the call today was another put-up job, to try to get him there.

Well, now, Remo had an edge. The man who was behind it all had wanted Remo to come; but he could not be sure that Remo was coming. Surprise might be on Remo's side.

CHAPTER NINETEEN

There was something wrong with the entire thing, Chiun thought, as he moved speedily, but not even seeming to move, through the crowd milling around at the United Nations building.

There had been too much advertising of the attack upon the delegates to the antiterrorist conference. Too many people knew. Dr. Smith knew and in his present state that might mean that half the people in the United States government knew. Remo knew. Chiun knew. That poor, simple girl knew.

It was not the way the thing should have been done. For was it not one of the precepts of Sinanju that the ideal attack must be quiet, merciless and unexpected? And this one violated all those rules, but especially the most important one—being unexpected. If one wished to assassinate the delegates to an antiterrorist conference, one did not wait until they were assembled behind the protective screen of thousands of policemen and special agents and what have you. One assassinated them in their beds, upon planes, in taxicabs, in restaurants, all more or less upon a given signal. The Americans had a proverb for it too, although he thought it might have been Korean: do not put all your eggs in one basket.

Perhaps Chiun was guilty of error; might he be overestimating the quality of their opponent? He thought about this as he moved. No, he had not. Their student was himself an adept at the secrets of Sinanju. There was no way that he would move stupidly.

And yet there had been much seeming stupidity in everything done thus far.

Chiun put the question behind him as he moved closer to the entranceway to the U.N. building, sifting through policemen and guards and other people whose eyes lacked the power to fix upon his motion.

It was easy to see Smith's men. He and Remo had joked, but they were right. Smith's men wore trench coats and hats with press cards in them, and carried cameras which they aimed at the crowds, without ever bothering to depress the shutters. And yes, there was Smith too, clad the same way, up on the steps of the building. Chiun shook his head. Oh well, he would be sure not to hit anyone wearing a trench coat.

Now—where would the attack on the delegates come from?

Deception was the keystone of everything that had been done so far. The attack would not be frontal. The assassins would be disguised.

Chiun looked around him. As newsmen? No, no one trusted newsmen, and policemen in emergency situations delighted in abusing them and demanding credentials. Perhaps as policemen? No, there were too many policemen who would have the opportunity to see through such disguises. As clergymen? No. There would be no reason for a group of clergymen to gather. Their presence alone would be suspicious.

Chiun looked around. Who could pass through the lines without question? Without the press interfering with them, without the police stopping them?

Of course.

He began to move toward the right edge of the plaza in front of the building's main entrance, toward a group of Army officers who were now moving resolutely through the crowd, through the police lines, toward the building. Chiun knew. The assassins had come as a military detail, and no one would question them, until it was too late.

It was adequate, Chiun told himself, but he still wondered why the attack was to be handled this way. It was defective in concept, and their opponent should have known better.

The front steps of the Museum of Natural History were sealed off by ropes with signs posted: *closed today.*

Remo went down the pedestrian ramp to the slightly below-ground first floor level. The door there was locked also and with the heel of his hand, he smashed out the locking mechanism so that the door opened easily. Behind him, in the taxicab, P. Worthington Rosenbaum wondered whether or not to call the police, then remembered the fifty dollar tip the man had given him, and decided that anything that happened at the museum was not the business of P. Worthington Rosenbaum.

Although it was summer, it was cool and dark in the building. Remo took a few steps forward across the highly polished marble floors into the central first floor reception hall. A long-ago memory told him that stairs were to the left and right of the passageway. In a small office on the corner of the first floor, a bearded young man sat, with a phone to his ear.

"He's here," he hissed.

He nodded as the voice came back: "Good. Follow him to the top floor. Then kill him."

"But suppose he doesn't go to the top floor?"

"He will. And when you are done with him, call me," the voice said, almost as an afterthought.

Remo moved to the stairs and started up. He would have to begin at the top floor; that reduced the chance of the prey escaping. It was one of the things Chiun had taught him.

On the top floor of the museum, the stairs led into a corridor at the end of which stood the dinosaur room. Remo moved into the room and looked around. There was brontosaurus, as he had remembered him as a child. He moved through the big, high gallery. There at the end was T. Rex, still evil and powerful looking although only a skeleton, towering high over Remo. This was the place. This entire building. The place of dead animals.

Remo heard a sound behind him and turned as the bearded youth came through the door corridor, clad all in black, wearing a black *gi*, a karate costume which in white is a formal attacking uniform, but in black is an affectation.

"Well, if it ain't the Cisco kid," Remo said.

The bearded man wasted no time. With a deep rumble of sound in his throat, he was in the air moving toward Remo, his leg tucked under him to unleash a kick, his right hand cocked high overhead to deliver a crushing hand mace.

The leap was long and high, right out of Nureyev. The conclusion was pure Buster Keaton. Before he could fire off a blow with either hand or foot, his throat ran into Remo's upthrust hand. The hardened heel buried itself deep in the man's Adam's apple. The bone and cartilage turned to mush under the hand and the man's leap stopped, as if he were a soft tomato plopping against a brick wall. He dropped heavily to the marble floor, without even a gasp or a groan.

So much for Cisco.

When the telephone had not rung in three hundred seconds, the small yellow man on the second floor smiled, and looked at Joan Hacker.

"He has breached our first line of defense," he said.

"You mean?"

"Our man in black is dead. Yes," the yellow man nodded.

"Why, that's terrible," Joan said. "How can you be so calm? That's just awful."

"Spoken like a true revolutionary. We capture airplanes and shoot hostages. Fine. We shoot unsuspecting athletes. Fine. We bring about the death of an innocent old butcher. Fine. We prepare this morning to kill a score of diplomats. Fine. But we should worry about the life of one high school dropout, whose karate technique was, to tell the truth, abysmal."

"Yes, but those other people are just . . . well, they're the enemy . . . agents of reactionary Wall Street imperialism. And the man downstairs . . . well, he was our man."

"No, my dear," the yellow man said. "They are all the same. They are all men. No matter what label they bear, they are all men. Only the unthinking and the unmerciful label them as agents of this or that, and then only so that they can justify their own refusal to treat each of them as a man. It is a greater justice to

161

kill a man, knowing full well that you are killing a man and not just ripping off a label. It gives meaning to that man's death and richness to one's own accomplishment."

"But that flies in the face of our ideology," Joan sputtered.

"As well it might," the yellow man said. "Because in this world, there is no ideology. There is only power. And power comes from life."

He stood up behind the small desk and leaned forward to Joan, who inexplicably recoiled in her seat. "I will share with you a secret," he said. "All these preparations, all these deaths, all have been undertaken with one purpose in mind. Not the glorification of some lunatic revolutionary ideal; not the bringing to power of unlettered savages whose unworthiness to rule is proven by their willingness to follow where ideology leads. Everything you and I have done has had only one purpose: the destruction of two men."

"Two men? You mean, Remo and the old . . . the old Oriental?"

"Yes. Remo, who would take unto himself the secrets of our ancient house, and Chiun, the elderly Oriental as you call him, who is the reigning Master of Sinanju and whose existence will always stand between me and my goals."

"I don't think that's revolutionary a bit." Joan Hacker sniffed. Suddenly she did not like this at all. It wasn't noble, like liberating an airplane or bombing an embassy. It was like murder.

"The man who wins can apply any labels he wishes," the yellow man said, his hazel eyes glinting. "Enough now. He will soon be here."

162

The fourth floor was empty and so was the third. Remo thought of the last time he had seen the museum, many years before. Remo was just another faceless kid in a crowd of orphans, who had never seen anything. It was back before cultural enrichment was considered an alternative to learning to read and write, and it was only when the entire class had mastered reading and writing that the nuns agreed to take them to the museum. Then it had been packed and noisy, but today it was empty and still, cold drafts were sweeping down the high broad corridors and stairwells, and it seemed a fitting place for the legend of the dead animals to end.

Remo remembered how the entire class had suffered and waited while Spinky, the class idiot, had suffered through reading lessons until he finally grasped the concept of words. Every day had seemed like a month. Well, Spinky was long behind him now; so was Newark and the orphanage and his childhood. All that was left of the Remo who had been was a first name. Not even a face or a random fingerprint existed to say that he had been here. And now as he moved smoothly down the wide twisting flight of steps to the second floor, he thought he would trade in everything to be back in the orphanage, to be wearing one dollar surplus Army sneakers along these halls, instead of thirty-four-dollar leather tennis shoes.

He stopped in the middle of the last flight of steps. At the bottom stood a big black man, wearing a dashiki. He looked up at Remo with a smile, then began up the stairs. Remo backed up until he was on the landing, midway between the third and second floor.

Right. He thought so. Another big black man was heading down on him from the third floor.

"Howdy," Remo said. "Ah come to jine up with yo third world."

"*Ave atque vale*," one of the men said. "That mean, hail and farewell," the other said.

"Good," Remo said. "Now do you know the 'Whiffenpoof Song'? If you want, I'll hum a few bars. Let's see. *Through the tables down at Morey's* . . . or is it *to the tables*. Anyway, it goes, *la, da, da, da, to the place where Louie dwells. . . .*" To their blank look, Remo said, "Don't know that one, huh? How about 'The Crawdad Song'? If you sing it, I'll yodel in the high spots."

Remo's back was now against the marble wall on the landing. It felt cold against his back, through his thin shirt, and he tensed his muscles against it, feeling them writhe against the stone.

Then the two big men were in front of him, and without warning, they fired heavy fists at his face. Remo paused, waited, then slid under the two punches. Rather than hit the wall with their fists, the men recoiled, but Remo was now between and behind them. He leaped into the air, and then flailed back with both elbows. Each elbow hit the back of a head, and the force of Remo's blows drove the faces forward into the unyielding cold marble. He heard two separate sets of cracks: one set as his elbows hit the men's skulls; the second set as their faces splashed and broke against the stone wall.

He stepped away without looking and heard them sink to the floor behind him. Then he was moving down the stairs again, three at a time.

At the bottom of the stairs, he stopped and then he heard it. Clap, clap, clap. A small and delicate round of applause. He looked to his left. Nothing. He moved to the right, following the sound, until he stood before the open doors leading to a large gallery. A broad balcony ran around the gallery, overlooking the first floor. Standing in front of him, near the stairs that led down to the well of the gallery, was Joan Hacker. And with her. . . . Remo grinned. He had been right. It was Nuihc.

He stopped clapping as his hazel eyes met Remo's deep brown ones.

"I knew it was you," Remo said.

"Did Chiun not tell you?" Nuihc asked.

Remo shook his head. "No. He has this funny idea that your name is not to be mentioned except in a funeral service. Something about your being a disgrace to his teaching and to his House."

"Poor old Chiun," Nuihc said. "In different times, in different circumstances, my father's brother would have been quite a man to know. But now, he is simply . . . well—out of it, to use your idiom."

Remo shook his head. "I have a hunch that the graveyards of the world are filled with men who decided that Chiun was out of it."

"Yes. But none of them are named Nuihc. None of them is blood of Chiun's blood. None of them is from the House of Sinanju. And none of them. . . ."

"None of them is a traitor to his heritage; none of them the kind of animal who recruits these poor mindless things to murder and rape for him. Why, Nuihc? Why terrorism?" Remo asked.

Joan Hacker's eyes had followed their conversation

165

as if it were a tennis match. Now she turned again from Remo, as Nuihc laughed. He leaned back against the marble railing and laughed heavily, a high piercing laugh that reminded Remo eerily of Chiun's high-pitched cackle. As he threw his head back, Remo could see behind him the cables holding the ninety-foot replica of the giant blue whale, largest animal ever to live on earth. The whale's shadow darkened the room.

"You still do not know, do you, white man?" Nuihc asked.

"Know what?" Remo said. And for the first time, he was uneasy.

"None of this has anything to do with terrorism. Did Chiun not tell you of the dog that barks and the dog that bites?"

"So?"

"So all the terrorism has been the dog that barks. The dog's bite was aimed at you and your aged friend. You two were the targets. Everything was aimed to that end. The plane whose hijackers insisted that they go to Los Angeles. That was so that I could be sure your government would call you in. The attack on the airport and the attack on the three colonels. Designed to bring you in closer and closer, deep into the target ring."

"It's one thing to name a target," Remo said. "It's another to hit it."

"But that is the beauty of it," Nuihc said. "You will hit it for me. You have no doubt dispatched poor Chiun to the United Nations, there to save the lives of diplomats whose lives are worthless. And there Chiun will do what Masters have been trained to do. He will move into and among the enemy. And then,

166

too late, he will find that not the diplomats, but he himself, is the target." Without looking at the watch he wore on his delicate wrist, Nuihc said: "It is ten forty-two. We can watch if you wish."

He motioned to Joan Hacker, who stepped aside and turned on a small battery-operated television set which was propped on the marble railing that ran around the balcony. The sound came on instantly—the roar of people chanting—and seconds later, the picture swirled on, showing the crowd milling about in front of the United Nations building, held back by squads of uniformed New York police.

As Remo watched, he saw, with a sinking feeling, the figure of Dr. Harold W. Smith, moving around behind the police lines. But there was no sign of Chiun.

The announcer's voice said: "The diplomats from the major countries all have arrived now and are inside. The conference should soon begin. But the mood of the crowd is growing uglier by the moment and we understand that police reinforcements are being sent to the scene. We now switch to our pool cameras inside the meeting chambers."

The camera blanked, and then another camera picked up the inside of the assembly chambers where the antiterrorist meeting would be held. It was mostly empty, although the few gallery seats were already filled. A few second-string diplomats sat at chairs, and young aides scurried in and out, carrying papers and notebooks, placing them at different desks.

There was only a hushed buzz from the gallery as the camera watched and then another announcer's voice intoned: "You are looking at the main assembly

167

chamber where today's conference on terrorism will be held. All is in readiness for the meeting which is expected to begin in another fifteen minutes. While the crowd outside is growing unruly, the feeling of diplomats here is that this is a great step forward for the forces of humanity in. . . ."

His voice was punctuated by a couple of sharp reports. Two. Then three. Then a fusillade of what were obviously bullets. The announcer's voice again: "We don't know what's going on here, and we don't wish to alarm anyone unduly. But those certainly sounded like shots. I'm going to try to find out what happened, and in the meantime, we'll return you outside."

The screen blanked again and Nuihc began to laugh.

"Goodbye, dear Uncle Chiun," he said, cackling, and then nodded his head to Joan Hacker to turn off the television. He looked now at Remo.

"You now look at the new Master of Sinanju," Nuihc said.

Remo just stared.

"Do you not see? Are you so blind? Everything was geared for this moment. It was essential to produce a new level of skill in terrorism; that was the only way to assure that your government would assign you and Chiun the task of stopping me. That was why the trick of bringing the weapons onto the planes, past the new metal detectors. Did you wonder how I did it?"

"Anyone could have figured it out," Remo said, dully, his mind now whirling in confusion, in shock at the thought of Chiun dead.

"Yes, but no one did. Metal detectors are designed by definition to detect hidden metal. We brought the weapons aboard planes in the open, mounted onto obvious metal objects that people are psychologically used to not inspecting."

Remo thought for a moment; the thing had gnawed at his mind. "The wheelchair," he said.

"Of course," Nuihc said. "The wheelchairs were reinforced with weapons parts. No one likes to look at a wheelchair, so no one examines it closely. And of course, since it is metal, it shows up as metal on the metal detector. And no one pays it any attention. Clever, was it not?"

"A parlor trick," Remo said. "You should see what John Scarne can do with a deck of cards."

"You deprecate my skills," Nuihc said. "Think of the training. The instant competence. Did Chiun explain that competence can be bestowed easily, if the trainee is expendable? You can make him able to deal with a few simple things very well. But that flash of training breaks down the moment anything unforeseen or unexpected enters into the mission."

"Chiun told me of the assault on the mountain," Remo said.

"Of course," Nuihc responded. "Those peasants were given instant competence. But their inability to imagine being inside a castle was the surprise. And so they all died. And then I sent the warnings. First fat, then thin, then the dead animals. It was to let Chiun know who his opponent was."

"Why?" Remo asked.

"So he would worry more about you and less about himself. He has . . . he had a strong instinct for survival, that one. It was necessary to disarm him by fragmenting his concentration."

169

"And then you had Joan here give me clues to get me here?" Remo asked.

"Yes. And that was the riskiest part. I knew that Chiun would not tell you of me, because he knew that would force you to prove your manhood by coming after me. I had to make you think you discovered me. So the clues could not be too blatant, lest you fear a trap. Yet, if they were too subtle, you would not understand them. That is not to downgrade you. It is the way with your western mind. And so you figured out what I wished you to figure out, and so you came, leaving Chiun alone to meet his death. And now you must decide."

"Decide what?" Remo asked.

"Will you join me? You have had experience working with the Master of Sinanju. Will you not now join the new Master as we move toward power over this globe?"

"And who elected you the new Master?" Remo asked coldly.

For a moment, Nuihc looked perplexed. Then he smiled and said, "There is no other."

"You're wrong," Remo said. "If Chiun is dead—which I doubt—if Chiun is dead, then I claim the seat of the House of Sinanju. I am the Master."

Nuihc laughed. "You forget yourself. You are only a white man, and I am not those cretins you have met with out in the hallways."

"No, you're not," Remo said. "They were just poor simpletons, like this dumb child here. But you? You're something else, you are. You're a mad dog."

"Then," Nuihc said, "the lines are drawn. But tell me, do you not feel a tinge of fear in your stomach when you remember the beating I gave you when last we met. I told you then that in ten years you would be magnificent. Ten years have not passed."

"And finally, dog meat, you've made a mistake," Remo said. "It wasn't to be ten years. Chiun told me. We were this much apart." He held up his fingers, separating his thumb and index finger by only a quarter-inch. "Just this much. Chiun thought five years. And then he admitted he had been wrong. I came on faster than he thought; he told me I was better than you. How does it feel to be a perpetual also-ran, dog meat? All your life, Chiun was better than you. And now, when you say you've gotten rid of him, I'm better than you. It's all over, Nuihc. And I'm not bound by a vow not to kill someone from the village."

Nuihc's face moved, showing the tension underneath. Remo waited. He did not know if Chiun was dead or alive, but if he was dead, if Nuihc's evil scheme had worked, then this moment of Remo's life would be dedicated to the Master's memory. He reached deep into the dark corners of his mind for words he had heard Chiun say, and intoned softly:

"I am created Shiva, the Destroyer, death, the shatterer of worlds. The dead night tiger made whole by the Master of Sinanju. What is this dog meat that now challenges me?"

Nuihc screamed, deep in his throat, the wail of a cruel, evil cat, and then leaped toward Remo.

171

CHAPTER TWENTY

Yes, there was definitely something wrong. The attack was wrong. Nuihc had planned it, but he had not planned it the way it should have been planned to be effective. And that gnawed at Chiun, as he fell in and disappeared among the small crowd of Army officers that moved imperiously through the police lines and toward the front entrance of the United Nations building.

The idea of using Army uniforms as a shield was good, Chiun thought. Only a trained eye would have looked past the silver and gold and braid and ribbons to see that some of the faces were pale around the chin, where beards had only recently been shaved off, and the skin under had not yet had time to darken. Only a very trained eye might notice that there was among the group a little more swarthiness than one could expect in a group of twelve American army officers.

But that is what was wrong. A trained eye would notice those things, and Nuihc should know that a trained eye would be looking for them. He would know that Remo and Chiun would be here, watching, and their eyes would not overlook the evidence of the recently-made-hairless faces and the swarthiness.

Unlike Nuihc to be so careless. But was it carelessness? Or was it something else?

Chiun shook his head slightly. And there was Remo to worry about. The child was not always sensi-

172

ble, risking death when he was free to depart. Not that the danger was that terrible. If Nuihc should harm Remo, he would spend the rest of his days in hiding or in flight, because the Master of Sinanju would track him to earth and Chiun's vengeance would be implacable and terrible to see. Surely, Nuihc would know this. So again, why would he use such childish means as hints and telephone calls, to entice Remo to come after him? Perhaps there was something else on Nuihc's mind. There were many things Chiun could not understand.

Chiun passed within inches of Dr. Smith who was marching back and forth, balefully staring at the crowd. He seemed to be trying to focus his eyes. Poor Dr. Smith. Chiun hoped that he would regain his senses before it was all too late.

Chiun seemed to drift in and out among the Army officers, at first visible, then gone, visible, then gone, so that there was no steady vision of him that a guard or a policeman could have moved to intercept. Instead, he was here, in bright sunshine, in front of 20,000 people—like an apparition, an afterglow, which vanishes between one blink and the next.

He was past the guards now and moving briskly with the Army contingent along the corridors of the United Nations building, toward the sections in the back where the main Assembly room was and which was bordered by conference rooms, small meeting rooms and offices.

The group of Army officers was led by a tall, sandy-haired man in his mid-forties who wore the stars of a major general on a pale tan gabardine suit. He carried an attaché case, as did all the men with him, and now

173

the general turned to look over his men, and he saw Chiun's face. Chiun met his eyes, but the general said nothing and made no acknowledgement. Instead, he led the way into a small room alongside the main Assembly hall. Chiun was in the middle of the group as they moved into the room.

Why had not the general acknowledged Chiun's existence? It was almost as if he had expected the Master to be there.

The last man into the room locked the door behind them, and now the men moved quickly. They began to peel off their Army uniforms. Underneath, they wore light blue shirts. From their attaché cases, they took thin silk robes which they slipped on, and burnooses which they placed on their heads. And finally handguns.

And all the while Chiun watched, as the men moved wordlessly. Handguns? Why? Why not explosives? Or gas? Why have gone this far to risk all on the poor marksmanship of one's men? Handguns were for single targets in enclosed areas; not for broad masses of men in a big open assembly room. Only for single targets in enclosed areas.

And then Chiun knew.

The diplomats who were to meet outside in minutes were not the targets of these assassins.

There was only one target, and he *was* in an enclosed area. The target was Chiun and he was now locked in the room with the twelve armed men who planned to kill him. And Remo would be at Nuihc's mercy. Nuihc would not hesitate to kill, because he knew that his own men would have killed Chiun.

The anger rose in his throat like a roar. The Master of Sinanju did not die like that. For the sin of arrogance, Nuihc would bleed longer than was necessary before Chiun took his full measure of justice.

Chiun's eyes met those of the man who had worn the general's stars. He was wearing now a thin red silk robe with a silver moon on its chest, and a silver burnoose, and he held a .45 automatic pointed at Chiun's chest. With a smile, he touched his hand to his chest, his forehead, and then moved it toward Chiun in the traditional Arabic *salaam,* but his mistake was moving his hand toward Chiun.

Chiun took the hand in flight and wheeled with it. The big man's body followed and he went over Chiun into a pile of men, all of whom had faced Chiun with drawn weapons.

And then Chiun was among them.

"You dare?" his voice shrieked, as his hands and arms and feet wreaked destruction on the men in the room. Shots fired. Two. Three. Then a fusillade, but Chiun was among the men and he could not be hit. He grabbed burnooses and men whirled, by their headpieces—crashing into others, and downing them like bowling pins.

"You dare?" Chiun screamed again, and while the men in the room paid the first installment of the price of his anger, the anger was at Nuihc first, but then also at himself, because he had let himself be fooled, and had allowed Remo to go, perhaps to his death. Because, in a battle of even strengths, the one who planned would win.

There were more shots, scattered, and than a final desperate salvo, and then there were no more shots

175

because there were no more men left alive to fire the guns. And when the door opened and security men poured through, Chiun moved silently through them, out into the corridor, and one of the men asked, "Did you see an old guy?" and the other said, "For Christ sake, how could anybody get past us?"

There might still be time. Nuihc, secure in the knowledge of Chiun's death, might dally with Remo; he might try pain; he might keep Remo alive for minutes, for even hours, to savor his triumph. There might still be time.

In the hall, Chiun saw a familiar figure running toward him. It was Dr. Smith.

"Chiun," he said. "I just realized. The Army officers. What happened?"

"They will kill no one, Dr. Smith."

"The diplomats are safe?"

"The diplomats were always safe. The assassins came for me, and they found me. Now, quickly. Where in this city are there dinosaurs to be found?"

"Dinosaurs?"

"Yes. Ancient reptiles who no longer walk the earth."

Smith hesitated and Chiun snapped, "Quickly. Unless you want yet another death on your hands."

"The only dinosaurs I ever saw are in the Museum of Natural History."

"And that is near here?"

"Yes."

"Thank you. Remo will be glad you are again well."

Chiun was gone. Out in front, the mob still surged and swelled against the police lines as rumor and word began to filter out that there had been deaths inside. But Chiun was through the lines and then the crowd, without ever touching a shoulder to another's body. A half-block away, a taxicab was stopped in traffic. It was empty. Chiun opened the front door and slipped into the front seat.

The driver turned to look at him and Chiun impaled him with his eyes. Then, glancing at the driver's registration over the windshield, he said: "P. Worthington Rosenbaum, you will take me to the Museum of Natural History. You will ride on the sidewalk if necessary to get me there rapidly. You will make no conversation if you wish to live. If you do all these things well, you will be rewarded. Now go."

P. Worthington Rosenbaum decided at that moment that he was leaving the taxi business, and going into partnership in a yarn shop with his sister. But first, he would get rid of this last half-a-deck at the Museum of Natural History.

As he tromped on the gas pedal, Chiun sat back in the seat. The ancient legend said that one typhoon was still when another passed. Well, Chiun still moved and if Nuihc began to roar, he would find the truth of the old legend that said one typhoon must die. In the place of dead animals.

CHAPTER TWENTY-ONE

It was very strange, what they were talking about. She was sure it was very significant. But the cocaine had made it so hard to concentrate. It was nice and dreamy. The whole world was nice and dreamy. It was wonderful being a revolutionary heroine.

But there were so many things she did not understand.

Nuihc—it was funny that he had never told her his name before—had said that Remo and the old gook were targets. But he must have been fooling, because the whole filthy exploitive capitalist system was the target. Of that, she was sure. Nuihc was as dedicated to the cause of the righteous revolution of the oppressed as she was. Without any doubt.

But then Remo had shown up and had said that he was the Master of Sinanju, whatever that was. And they had talked about the old man as if he had died.

And why did they want to watch things on television? Television. It *would* be nice to see what was happening to those imperialist running dogs up at the United Nations.

All this chitter-chatter between Remo and Nuihc wasn't very interesting anyway. Typhoons. Barking dogs. Tricks. Guns in wheelchairs.

Silly, all of it. All that counted was a new order for the Third World. She had been willing to step aside, once the revolution was accomplished, but now she wondered if she should. She might just be the kind of

178

leader that they would need. After all, what did they know of government, the poor, naked, ignorant savages?

From the corner of her eye, she saw Nuihc leap at Remo, just as she turned the television back on. The announcer's voice was a backdrop for the sound of their scuffle.

She watched, suddenly realizing this was a battle to the death. Goodie. She felt like Queen Guinevere. Was that her name? Yes. Arthur's wife.

Nuihc was very good. He threw a punch which seemed to be in slow motion, but it hit Remo and it spun him around. Remo was bigger and stronger, but maybe he was slower. He threw a blow that missed, and he slid past Nuihc toward the marble balcony railing that overlooked the first floor and the huge suspended whale.

Nuihc clasped both his hands together over his head, like a prizefighter in victory, and jumped toward Remo who lay sprawled across the railing. But Remo rolled away, just as Nuihc's hands crashed down and hit the railing with a crack like a pistol shot. The marble chipped and fell to the floor.

Then Remo was standing on the railing, and then Nuihc hopped onto the railing too. Back and forth they moved, each throwing blows, each missing. Remo did something fancy with a kick that missed, and his momentum took him off the railing and he plunged toward the floor thirty feet below, but he caught onto one of the overhead cables that supported the fiberglass replica of the ninety-foot whale, and turning his body in the air, did a double flip and landed on his feet on the whale's back, twenty-five feet above the floor.

Nuihc dove for the cable, also spun in the air, and landed softly on the back of the whale five feet from Remo.

And then they fought back and forth along the back of the whale. Strange, they had fought and fought and fought, and yet she found it hard to remember either of them landing a hard blow. Perhaps they weren't really very good after all.

She ignored the buzz of the television as she watched. She squealed. Fight on, men. My heart to the winner.

Then somehow Remo had Nuihc's two wrists in his hands and was squeezing. Nuihc pulled back and then lunged forward. His body twisted in the air, and his feet went up and over Remo's head.

How wonderful. They were fighting over her. She felt like throwing a kerchief so they could fight for it and the winner could pin it over his heart. But she didn't have a kerchief. She had a Kleenex. It was wet. She threw that. It didn't go very far.

Nuihc landed behind Remo, his back to Remo, and his hands were free, his body carefully balanced, but before he could turn, the wet Kleenex fluffed through the air, hit his shoulder, and Joan giggled as it plopped on the whale's back. The small touch of the crumpled paper destroyed Nuihc's balance and he slid to the back of the whale. Before he could regain his feet, Remo was on him with an elbow.

And then Remo lifted Nuihc by the scruff of the neck and carried him like a suitcase toward the head of the whale.

The winner and champion. He had fought for Guinevere and won. Too bad. She had hoped Nuihc would be her savior. Oh, well. At least, she and Remo were sexually compatible.

"Hey, toots," Remo called. "Turn up the sound on that television, will you?"

CHAPTER TWENTY-TWO

Remo tied Nuihc's hands behind his back with Nuihc's own leather belt, then hung him from the whale's mouth, his hands and arms pulled up painfully behind him.

Then he almost skipped the distance down to the floor, landing softly on his feet, not even pausing to brace himself, but hitting—click—and stepping off in a fast trot.

He came up the stairs and stood alongside Joan Hacker, who was amusing herself by stuffing a little cocaine inside her upper lip.

"Want a snort?" she giggled.

"No thanks," he said. "I prefer rice myself."

"Oh, rice must be nice, but I've never sniffed it. Anyway, you've won. My body is yours."

"Stuff your body into your mouth and silence it, will you? I'm trying to hear the television."

The announcer was talking.

"There is still only confusion here. The crowd outside remains more or less under control, but we have definitely confirmed that shots were fired inside the U.N. building. However, we are advised that no diplomats . . . we repeat, no diplomats . . . have been shot. The victims of the shooting appear to have been a group of Army officers, but there is some question as to their identity. We are awaiting further details."

Remo snarled at the television. Maybe this and maybe that. Confusion and further details. He wanted to shout: *Is Chiun all right?*

There was a groan from the direction of the whale. Remo turned and his eyes met Nuihc's, as the small Oriental was hung out, like a side of beef from the jaw of the huge whale replica.

His eyes screamed hatred for Remo.

"If it had not been for her, I would have won," he hissed.

"Just a theory on your part," Remo said. "Now for a fact. I don't know yet whether Chiun is all right or not. But if he is not, I'm going to come back and peel your skin off in strips. You better hope your men missed."

Remo turned on his heel to walk away.

"You can't go," Joan Hacker shrieked. "You've won me. You have to take my body now."

"I might have your body but I know your soul will always belong to the Third World."

"No, Remo," she said. "Not any more. I'm tired of the Third World. I want to go home. I want you to take me home."

Suddenly, she was a very young girl again, as cocaine depression seized her.

Remo felt sorry for her. "I've got to find something out first," he said. "Then I'll take you home."

He walked away and as he went down the stairs, he heard Nuihc's voice behind him, speaking softly to the girl.

Remo cracked open the front door of the museum and stepped out onto the broad stone stairway that led down to the street.

From far down the block, he heard the *whoop, whoop, whoop* of sirens. From the rising pitch, he

183

could tell they were heading his way. He looked, and then saw a familiar looking yellow cab, careening down the street, between cars, bouncing off curbs, racing toward him. Several blocks behind it were a string of squad cars, strung out, following the maniacal cabdriver.

Then the taxi pulled abreast of Remo, hopped the curb up onto the sidewalk, and skidded to a stop. The passenger's door opened and Chiun stepped out on the sidewalk.

"Now, begone, P. Worthington Rosenbaum," he said to the driver. The cabbie took off again down the street and only seconds later, the police cars roared by in full pursuit. Chiun looked up, saw Remo on the top of the stairs, paused, then smiled.

He strolled casually up the stairs, hitching his robes up around his ankles.

"Kind of in a hurry to get here, Little Father?" Remo said.

Chiun looked at him blandly. "You have no doubt forgotten the importance of this day?"

"Importance?"

"Today is the day we are to visit Brooklyn."

"Oh," Remo said, snapping his fingers. "No wonder you were in a hurry."

"Of course," Chiun said. "What else could be so important that I would rush anywhere?"

Remo nodded. "Well, before we go, I want you to see something. I have a present for you."

He turned and led the way into the museum, through the great entrance hall, up the stairs and into the back gallery where the whale hung.

He flung back his arm dramatically toward the

whale, stepped back so Chiun could see and said, "There."

"There what?"

Remo turned. Only the belt still hung from the whale's open mouth. Nuihc was gone. Remo ran to the steps and looked down into the gallery. On the floor at the bottom lay the sprawled figure of Joan Hacker.

Remo ran down the stairs to her and turned her over. Her face had been split open. Blood poured from a fracture near her temple and jagged pieces of bone protruded through her fresh young skin.

"Nuihc did it," she gasped. "When you left, he said he loved me. He needed me for his revolution. I climbed down and untied him. Then when I got down, he hit me."

Remo looked at the wound and knew that Nuihc could have killed her instantly had he chosen. He had chosen to kill her slowly. Why?

"Did he tell you anything? To tell me?" Remo asked.

"He said to tell you he would be back. And the next time you would not be so lucky."

She groaned. "Remo?"

"Yes, Starlight."

"Why did he hit me? Didn't he want me with him in the new world?"

And because he did not want to hurt her any more, Remo tried to find an answer. Finally, he said, "He knew I loved you. He could see it in my eyes. He just didn't want to lose you to me, or to my side."

"Would your side have me?"

"Any side would be happy to have you," Remo said.

Joan Hacker smiled broadly, showing a newly capped upper right frontal bicuspid, and died in Remo's arms.

Remo had once seen a picture, painted by Hyacinthe Kuller, of a young girl asleep, and as Joan's eyes drifted closed, he thought again of that picture and how Joan at last looked satisfied.

He put her down gently and looked up at Chiun.

"Should we chase him?" Remo asked.

"No. He is gone now. We have only to wait. When we want him, he will find us."

"When he does, Chiun, he's mine."

"Is it of any importance to me what two amateurs do to each other? I wish to keep you alive only long enough to take me to Brooklyn to visit the Streisand shrine."

"All right, all right, Chiun, enough, enough. Today. I promise."

But there were things to do first. Back at the apartment, Remo changed, and while he was in the bedroom, Smith appeared.

"The antiterrorist pact was approved by the nations today by a unanimous vote," he said to Remo, as he came from the bedroom door.

"Terrific," Remo said, sarcastically. "It won't do one damn bit of good. It's another piece of paper that governments will ignore or tear up whenever it suits their purpose."

"I'm sure the President will be interested in your viewpoints, particularly coming as they do from someone with such a rich background of international political experience." Smith sniffed, as if smelling

186

something bad, and Remo knew he was back to normal.

So Remo said, "Because you threw us a curve ball on this one and nearly got us killed with your meddling. . . ."

"Meddling?"

"Yes, meddling," Remo said.

"You are probably the only functionary in the world who thinks a superior's order is meddling."

"Have it your own way," Remo said. "Anyway, because of that, Chiun and I are going out to blow a month's pay."

"Oh? Should I know where you'll be?"

"We're going to Brooklyn," Remo said.

"It's impossible to blow a month's pay in Brooklyn," Smith said.

"Just watch us," Remo said.

By the time Remo was dressed and ready to leave, the afternoon news was on and the announcer was speaking cheerily of the antiterrorist pact which would serve to turn worldwide terrorists into hunted animals.

"The nations of the world today have served notice that civilized people will protect themselves from mad dogs, no matter under what political flag those mad dogs hide."

Halfway across a nation, Mrs. Kathy Miller watched the same newscast. She thought back now of the terror of only ten days ago. It all seemed as if it had happened to someone else, far back in the past. She remembered the rape and she remembered her dead baby, but strangely, equally strong were the memories of the good and gentle man who had sat next to her, and who had told her that life was beautiful and that those who believed in life would survive.

And for that moment, Mrs. Miller believed it. She stood, turned off the television set and went into the bedroom where her late-working husband still slept, determined to join with him in love, to create a new life in her body.

Watch for

DEATH THERAPY

the next AUTHORS' CHOICE BEST OF THE
DESTROYER
from Pinnacle Books

coming in April!

The Destroyer
Warren Murphy

CELEBRATING 10 YEARS IN PRINT
AND OVER 22 MILLION COPIES SOLD!

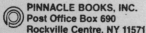